A DEADLY PREDICTION

A Leslie Sisters Mystery

Carola Goodman

Copyright 2012 by Carola Goodman
All rights reserved
Printed in the United States of America

ISBN: 1480119458
ISBN 13: 9781480119451

To the usual suspects with special thanks to

Marissa Rebecca and
Gabriella C.G. Seitter

CHAPTER ONE

"Oh, look Fall is officially here! Isn't it wonderful?" exclaimed Susana delightedly waiving a newspaper at Cornelia.

"Today is the tenth of October. If you hadn't noticed, Fall has been 'officially' here for the past three weeks," replied Cornelia dodging her sister's animated waving.

"Of course, silly, a first grader knows that.

What I meant was that the Halloween Festival is just around the corner! I really don't think of Fall until the announcement of the festival hits the paper. Funny isn't it?" Susana screwed up her brows in contemplation.

"Don't try to pull that air of innocence with me, Susana. As members of the Women's Institute we've both known about the festival for months now. Besides, Madame Sonia called this morning to say that your costume fitting has been changed to tomorrow at three o'clock."

Without missing a beat, Susana changed her expression and replied, "Oh drat, I was looking forward to seeing how my costume was coming along! Madame Sonia is really so talented, I don't know how she does it. Well, as the old saying goes, 'What can't be cured must be endured'. Now I'll have time to work on my chili recipe. I'm having such a hard time deciding what herbs to use - any ideas?"

Picking up the paper Cornelia read:

EPPING WOMEN'S INSTITUTE
ANNUAL HALLOWEEN FESTIVAL
Saturday, 31$_{st}$ October
CHILI COOK-OFF (new event!)
JACK-O-LANTERN LIGHTING
(all invited to bring their carved pumpkins)
HAUNTED MAZE
MASQUERADE BALL and COSTUME CONTEST

Sighing she said, "I suppose you'll be in your usual whirlwind of frantic activity for the next several weeks." Her words fell on an empty room as Susana was making her way to the kitchen to begin her test run of chili recipes. Before Susana entered the huge room full of the latest professional appliances, she stopped at the door and sniffed the air. A most unappetizing aroma of what she could only describe as burnt liver permeated the hall. If that wasn't enough, she swore there was a disgusting aroma of burning fish as well. Pushing the door open, her worst fears were confirmed. A weaker person with a more delicate constitution, e.g., a sailor, would have gagged and headed for the door. Not Susana. Impervious to the cook-housekeeper's oddball concoctions, not to mention her ability to come unhinged on a regular basis, Susana casually opened windows while managing desultory conversation with a placid smile.

"Is this a new recipe?" asked Susana fanning the smoke with her hand while peering into the pot that Martha was hunched over. Martha's red hair was in its usual tangled mess but now it was infused with a nauseating scent. Susana very deftly used the smokescreen to turn off the stove.

With the smoke cleared, Martha's red face showed clear signs of frustration. "If you must know the answer is yes and no. My ma used to make a tasty dish of liver 'n bacon that would knock yur socks off. I 'ad the recipe somewheres but it's disappeared so I'm experimentin'. Is that alright with you?" Then as an aside and looking straight at Susana she added, "Some people are always mindin' other folks' business."

With her trick of jumping in where angels fear to tread Susana replied, "Do I smell fish? When are you going to add the bacon?"

That's all it took for the cook-housekeeper to turn around, hands on hips and with a deprecatory look at her employer replied, "An' folks say you're a goormay? Do you smell bacon? 'Course not 'cause there ain't any! I said I was experimentin', didnt' I? A real cook, not a goormay, knows that fish is a substitute for bacon or any other kind 'a meat. Do I 'ave to learn you everythin'?"

Unfortunately for Susana, her stunned expression lasted a second too long resulting in more vituperation from Martha. "Now look what you've done askin' me all those fool questions. My chili's burnt almost through the pot! An' it would 'a won first prize too! I'm just gonna have to throw the whole thing out, includin' the pot! And if you think I'm fixin' up dinner tonight you're sadly mistakin'. Person can't stand in front of a stove all day!" She'd never know Susana's relief.

Dinner at Blandings, the Leslie family home, was a very animated affair thanks to Susana's having had the entire kitchen more or less to herself aided by the now very capable Pinkey. Some months prior, it had been arranged that Martha's sister's daughter,

Pinkey, would take over the cooking to give Martha more time to do her other duties. In all truth it had been a unanimous vote by the Leslie family that in deference to their health and well-being, Martha would have to be replaced as cook. Martha, remaining true to her always erratic behavior stayed in her room only setting foot in the kitchen every so often to grab some refreshment or as she put it, '*to keep an eye on the amatoors*'.

"Mmm, the corn chowder is delicious, Susana.

There wouldn't be any seconds, would there?" asked Jack sheepishly.

A pretty woman on his right laughed indulgently, "I honestly don't know where you put it. If I ate like you I'd be at least fifty pounds overweight. It's really not fair how men can eat 'til they burst and not show. But I agree Susana, the chowder's excellent and I could eat the entire loaf of bread in one sitting, which I might do if I don't take it back to the kitchen right now!"

Ann Grey and Jack Leslie had been recently married. Ann, with her several siblings, had been raised in St. James Woods, a village not far from Epping. A well-established family in the county, the Greys had close ties with the Leslie family. The younger generation had grown up together attending the same schools. Ann had been an excellent equestrian and her passion for the sport increased as she got older.

She had the wholesome good looks of an athlete with an easygoing personality. During the week she worked in a publishing firm in the City where she and Jack maintained a flat. However, she continued her equestrian training in Epping. Cornelia and Susana could not have been more delighted with Jack's new bride. They had grown up with her older siblings and now they welcomed Ann as a sister. Ann was also extremely happy with her new family, shrugging her shoulders with affable good humor at the eccentricities of her sisters-in-law. Blandings was not unfamiliar territory and she had no trouble fitting in.

Susana beamed happily. "I was having so much fun without Martha continually looking over my shoulder that I made two desserts: baked apples and chocolate brownies. It's not really that I mind Martha so much but she does make me a little nervous, if you know what I mean - do you?"

"Really girls, I don't know why you keep Martha on when she's nothing but trouble for you. It's not like she does any useful work or any work if it comes to that. She has two ways of cooking – burnt and raw, she has tantrums on a daily basis, and she's constantly giving notice. I just can't understand why you continue to put up with her," remarked Jack.

"Actually neither do we," replied Cornelia dispiritedly.

"Yes we do! It's because she's been with us so long that we don't notice her antics anymore – do we?" replied Susana.

Jack and Cornelia gave each other knowing looks. "Yeah, I suppose she's become a fixture here and she certainly provides a weird form of entertainment," Jack capitulated.

"That reminds me, Pinkey was telling me that Martha is making her Halloween costume out of pieces of cloth she's buying from the gypsies. I can't wait to see..." Susana wasn't allowed to finish her thought due to the simultaneous interruption from both her siblings.

"*Gypsies?*" asked Cornelia.

"Gypsies haven't been around here for ages!" remarked Jack.

"I seem to have heard something about them camping at Hunter's Bosk," replied his wife.

"Well they're back. Isn't it exciting? And just in time for Halloween! I wonder if they're the same ones who've been here before?" wondered Susana.

"After what happened in Hunter's Bosk last year you'd think Pinkey would stay well away from there – especially at night," remarked Cornelia.

"That was an isolated case, Cornelia. Nothing of that magnitude has ever happened in those woods as long as anyone can remember. We've all grown up playing in the Bosk and I'd hate to think that it would be branded as haunted just because of that one incident," said Jack with resolve.

"Do you have to be so gruesome, Jack? No one said anything about Hunter's Bosk being haunted.

And besides, I never liked going there even as a child. I always thought the trees had a way of looking like weird creatures, especially at night. Don't you think it's spooky?" appealed Susana.

Ann smiled and said "I know what you mean but I ride through those woods on a regular basis and they're as peaceful as they've always been – or almost always. I don't think you need to worry."

Not wanting to take sides, Cornelia replied, "Changing the subject, there was a very strange odor coming from the kitchen this morning. What did Martha burn today?"

"Ugh, don't remind me. It was really the worst combination of foods that I can remember her concocting. Martha is apparently going to enter the chili cook-off. I probably shouldn't tell you what she was cooking since we're at the dinner table but I will anyway. It was monkfish and liver! It was truly unappetizing and she blamed me for it burning!

Honestly, she should have thanked me – it makes me queasy just to think of it. Why would someone ever want to be a food judge?" replied Susana.

"Do I have to remind you of last year's disaster? Oh wait, last year *I* was made judge of the pumpkin pie contest when Lady Millicent became conveniently sick at the last minute. Yes, I must agree with you that Martha's original recipes, or to be more specific, everything she cooks is definitely unpalatable. And this year I flatly refuse to be duped into judging a food event again!" said Jack somewhat humorously.

"Do you remember how the face guard on your knight's helmet kept closing every time you tried to take a bite? It was hilarious!" gasped Ann trying to catch her breath.

"Ha, ha, laugh all you want but it came in handy. I didn't actually taste Martha's entry and it hid the expression of disgust on my face!"

CHAPTER TWO

By mid-October, the temperature had dropped significantly. The skies were overcast a good part of the time with large, swelling clouds and gusting winds.

Ever since they could remember, the Leslie children had celebrated Halloween in the village of Epping just as they had when they were across the pond in the U.S. The American side of the Leslies had brought Halloween to the village when the children were small and from then on it had become an annual celebration.

With an American father the Leslie children had a special fondness for Halloween. The villagers, both young and old, also grew to anticipate the holiday with its charming decorations and special events. Cornelia and Susana's attachment to Halloween had not lessened as they grew older. If anything, it became even more special. Jack on the other hand had outgrown the holiday in his mid-teens and now humored his sisters with his participation as he mockingly put it, 'for the honor of the family's Yankee blood'.

"Your desserts were delicious as always Susana. Now if you ladies will excuse me I'll take some of the brownies back to my study. I know that the three of you are itching to get on with your Halloween plans," remarked Jack with a wry grin.

"Gosh, I'd love to talk about Halloween but I had a particularly difficult ride today and I'm exhausted. Can we talk tomorrow at breakfast? I've an awesome idea for a costume," replied Ann joining her husband.

"He's such a stinker, you'd think he could read our minds. Shall we take our Ovaltine upstairs?" proposed Susana to Cornelia as their brother and his wife left.

It was a long established custom for the sisters to have their bedtime Ovaltine together when there was anything of concern and/or interest that they wished to discuss. The ritual of taking the comforting beverage to a place of succor at the end of the day had a soothing effect and made any worrisome matter seem a little less daunting.

As was their custom, they first went to Susana's room where Cornelia left her tray of Ovaltine and perhaps dessert on a small table beside a divan, then she went to her own room to wash up and change. Having gotten into her bed Susana spent the time propping up half a dozen pillows around the bed piled high with blankets and a pink satin comforter.

"It occurred to me that my costume is ruined! Now what am I going to wear?" exclaimed Cornelia slumping into the divan and throwing up her hands in despair.

"Oh dear, did you spill something on it? Don't tell me you put on some pounds because the way you run all over the village…"

Cornelia interrupted, "No it's not that. If the gypsies are in the village how can I wear a gypsy costume? I'm always a gypsy for Halloween! But I don't want to offend them with my costume," she declared in frustration.

"You could still be a gypsy Cornelia, why not borrow a *real* gypsy outfit from them? Nothing personal or anything but your costume is getting a little redundant year after year. Why not try for an authentic look? That couldn't possibly offend them – could it?" suggested Susana with a touch of hesitation in her voice.

"Hmm, that's not a bad idea. Do you suppose they would sell me an outfit? I wouldn't want to insult them by asking for one."

Susana's expression turned into one of alarm. "I hadn't thought of that. If they were insulted they might put a hex on you! Uh oh, maybe my idea wasn't very good after all. But of course that might just be an old wive's tale. I know, why not be a witch, you always liked that costume, didn't you?"

Taking a sip of her Ovaltine Cornelia chuckled, "Don't worry Susana, I'll figure it out. Now what about you? You've been unusually silent about your costume and it's got to be stunning if Madame Sonia's working on it. What are you going to be this year?"

"I'm not going to give it away. Everyone's going to be so surprised! Madame Sonia is a genius – she helped me come up with the idea. Would you believe that almost half the village has her working on costumes? She must be sewing night and day! Tomorrow's my last fitting–I got started early.

She's keeping it for me until the day of the festival so *it'll stay a secret*. Isn't it thrilling?"

"I'm sure it's going to be perfect and I can't wait to see it," replied her sister indulgently. Getting up and heading for the door, she continued, "Sleep tight and don't forget that tomorrow morning is the Women's Institute meeting. Apparently, they're hoping to finalize the plans for the festival."

CHAPTER THREE

The weather the following morning was a blend of sunshine and pleasant breezes giving the entire countryside an invigorating air. Taking advantage of this opportune gift, the Leslie sisters left Blandings on foot and placidly wound their way down the country lanes to the town hall where the W.I. meeting was to be held. Every so often one or the other would stop to admire the sights that make country living so special–a late blooming rose trailing over a cottage fence, a small nest now abandoned by its former residents, the colored carpet of autumn leaves beginning to cover the ground or a small animal scurrying along a hedgerow.

"I love this time of year. Doesn't everything glow in this light?" exclaimed Susana munching on a berry.

"You know, I bet the W.I. will ask us if the hay maze can be in our lower field now that the town is building a senior center in the public meadow."

"Why, that would be lovely! Just think, we wouldn't have to walk all the way to the meadow because it'll be right down our hill and it would be so much fun having a bird's eye view of the maze. I wouldn't get lost in there because I'd memorize the path – genius isn't it?"

"It's just a hunch I have Susana, nothing's been said or anything. And don't forget that Sam Taylor has a fallow field right now that could also be used. We'll just have to wait and see what happens.

Of course we'll have to get Jack's opinion, although I don't think he'll mind. My only concern is the crowds and how to keep them from roaming around the grounds. Oh well, we'll cross that bridge...as they say."

By the time the sisters arrived at the Epping town hall that was located on the village common, the hall was already bustling with women, some in small groups and all talking at the same time.

The Leslie family was held in affectionate esteem in the village due to their goodwill and unflagging support in all matters having to do with the village and its residents. They were great donors not only of their time but also financially, something that didn't go unnoticed and strengthened the village's admiration. Reaching the eighteenth century hall the sisters made their way to some empty chairs and took their places in readiness for the meeting. Within seconds, a woman dressed in tight fitting jeans and a very form-fitting sweater sat down in the empty chair next to Susana and immediately introduced herself.

"Howdy! I'm Edith Kramer. You must be Susana Leslie, so glad to meet you, and you must be Cornelia! I'm new to Epping but I'm trying to get to know everyone and everything about the place, it's so enchanting!" she said chattily, leaning over Susana to talk to Cornelia.

The American accent was undeniable and Cornelia smiled cordially as her sister welcomed the newcomer with profuse commentary on the merits of the village.

Excitedly nodding her head and making her huge dangling earrings shake and clang, the woman continued, "I was very lucky to find a long-term place to stay in this part of the world. I can't tell you how long I've been looking here. I finally found..."

She was interrupted in mid-sentence as Susana exclaimed, "Oh, you must be Mrs. Brown's new lodger! Such a lovely house! You'll be very comfortable there and Mrs. Brown is a wonderful cook. Isn't she Cornelia?"

"Yes, you're very lucky to have found a home with Mrs. Brown. Her family's been in Epping for decades."

"I guess I was at the right place at the right time. The house is *sooo quaint* and full of bric-a- bracs. Sooo charming. I'm looking forward to staying there a long time. She's a widow I believe?"

"That's right," replied Cornelia wondering how long it took to apply pancake makeup.

After several knocks from her gavel, Petra Aleman, the pretty blond chairwoman of the W.I. was able to get the attention of the assembly and the meeting was called to order.

"Welcome, everyone. Before our first order of business is conducted I would like to welcome Mrs. Edith Kramer, a new member of our organization," announced the chairwoman.

Almost before Mrs. Aleman had finished her sentence Edith Kramer stood up and waved enthusiastically at the smiling faces and friendly clapping. After several seconds had gone by the newcomer remained standing, working the audience with professional skill. It was after several throat clearings and loud coughs that a flustered Petra Aleman was able to get Edith Kramer to sit down and thereby regain the attention of her audience.

"Everyone's so friendly! All this commotion is a little embarrassing. I'm normally so reserved," explained Edith in a loud stage whisper, eliciting some giggles from those around her. With raised eyebrows Cornelia and Susana exchanged looks.

Thanking the Public Relations Committee for the very well received article in the 'Town Crier' announcing the Halloween Festival, the chairwoman proceeded to the first item on the agenda, which was the location of the very popular maze. A committee would be set up to gather information for its location.

As is typical in the countryside where the residents have known each other for years, formality was thrown aside and someone in the assembly stood up and volunteered that both the Leslie and Taylor properties were the only viable places in which to erect the maze. With justifiable enthusiasm, and to her sister's surprise, Susana quickly stood up and announced that it would be an honor to have the maze laid out on Leslie property.

"That was such a *generous* act! I'm sure that it's going to be *much nicer* there than on a smelly old farm. I can't wait to see your place!" announced Edith Kramer in hushed tones that carried across the room.

Noticing that they were the beneficiaries of amused looks from the villagers, Cornelia and Susana could only smile weakly in return.

Thinking that a touchy item was quickly averted, Petra Aleman gave an inward sigh of relief for the quick and convenient disposal of a precarious issue. However her good fortune was short-lived because almost at once a member stood up expressing an opinion that last year's maze had been too challenging. Other women chimed in declaring concerns about safety issues with respect to the size of the maze. Aware that several minutes could be saved while at the same time avoiding the eruption of a heated discussion, the chairwoman proposed that they move on to the creation of a maze committee.

"Having some experience in this field I would be happy to donate my time to chair the committee," pronounced Mrs. Kramer, standing up and looking around as if she were a general inspecting her troops. "Very...um...appreciated. But, you see, it's customary for the committee members to elect their chairwoman," replied a now even more flustered Petra Aleman after hearing several gasps and staring at a sea of angry faces.

"Don't worry about it Hon! I bet once the committee hears my ideas they'll elect me their leader. After all, we want it to be an unforgettable event!" replied Edith Kramer preening.

The 'Chili Cook-off' was next on the agenda.

This was a new and highly anticipated event brought about as a direct result of the popularity of this item on the menu of the village pub, The Raven's Roost.

Several villagers had at one time or another boasted of their own 'secret' chili recipes that, if not tastier, could give the pub owner's wife a run for her money.

Petra Aleman had been looking forward to this moment in order to make a special announcement She was gratified with loud applause when she announced that a London food writer had agreed to be the guest judge for the event.

Susana leaned over to her sister and whispered, "I'd like to volunteer for this committee but I wonder if the committee members can enter the contest – what do you think?"

Before Cornelia could reply, Edith Kramer's voice could be heard addressing the members. "Of course you all know that chili is *American* and it's obvious that *only* an *American* knows how real chili should *taste*. I want you all to know that I'm not going to enter the contest because clearly I have an advantage and that, in my opinion, wouldn't be kosher. *But*, I would be willing to share my knowledge and experience with any of the members so that this event can be a true chili cook-off in the best Texas tradition!" she ended scanning the crowd with a self-satisfied look.

The looks of sheer loathing on the faces of the W.I. members would not have been out of place in a prison for mass murderers.

In an effort to reduce the tension in the room and return the meeting to a semblance of normalcy, Susana raised her hand, and when acknowledged by the chairwoman asked about the rules for entry into the contest. After much debate, and a lot of grumbling, it was decided that entry to the chili cook-off would be open to everyone. It was not difficult for the chairwoman to enlist eager volunteers for the committee.

"I'm sure your chili won't need any tweaking –

I've heard about your reputation as a cook. But you know the old expression, '*There's always room for improvement*'!" said Edith Kramer with a shrill laugh.

Susana gave Edith a watery smile and edged closer to her sister.

The annual 'Jack-O-Lantern Lighting' was next on the agenda. Not a lot of time was spent discussing this event because it had become a tradition that the secretary of the W.I. would automatically take on the responsibility of overseeing the necessary functions of the competition with the help of one or two women. This was a very popular event, with the carved pumpkins set on bleachers on the village common. In the evening, to the delight of the villagers and many others, the bleachers would be filled with uniquely carved pumpkins, all lit and glowing into the wee hours of the night.

Petra Aleman, a thoroughly capable chairwoman, was able to keep the meeting under control with only a few mishaps and the last item on the agenda was brought up before the ladies of the W.I. Every year since its inception the Masquerade Ball and Costume Contest was the event that brought in the most profits for the W.I. For months the villagers would work on their costumes in eager anticipation.

As the seat of local government since the eighteenth century, the town hall also provided recreational space for the village. A vast room on the second floor was used both as a ballroom and a theatre. The stage with its elegant velvet curtains was a source of pride for the town. The principal duty of the committee in charge of overseeing the event was that of decorating and the placing of tables in an adjacent room for the gargantuan feast served later in the evening. It had been decided years before that the supper would be the responsibility of every person who bought a ticket for the Ball by bringing a savory or dessert. This was another opportunity for the various cooks to show off their talent with prized recipes. It was not uncommon for villagers to starve themselves all day in preparation for the enormous repast of the evening.

With mounting excitement a rolling murmur could be heard as several of the members became absorbed in discussing the previous year's costumes.

The stimulating and never-stale topic of who wore what along with analysis and commentary was a favorite topic amongst the ladies.

No less interested in this subject than their fellow members, Cornelia and Susana sat on the edge of their seats in animated conversation with three ladies seated in front of them.

"I can already tell that the Halloween festivities are going to be a *scream*! I've never heard more gossip and cattiness in all my life! This is going to be more fun than I thought!" shrilled Edith into Susana's ear, getting not only Susana's attention but that of all those around them as well.

Both sisters winced. Susana in pain and Cornelia at the contemptuous looks from their fellow W.I. members.

With several exasperated knocks from her gavel, the chairwoman was able to regain the attention of the group and the matter of setting up the committee took place. Surprisingly, and to Susana's horror, when the American attempted to give her opinions on the subject Susana pulled her back in her seat with a quick tug of her pants. The unfortunate Edith fell back as if stunned and then let out a loud guffaw with a conspiratorial wink at a horrified Susana.

CHAPTER FOUR

In an effort to avoid the hostile looks of the village women, Cornelia and Susana dashed for the exit directly after the first pound of the gavel ending the meeting. Unhappily, their attempt at a quick getaway was foiled when they were approached by several women and bombarded with questions asking if Edith Kramer was "...*a Leslie family friend from America?*"– this with dour expressions; "...*if there was an accompanying Mr. Kramer along with little Kramers?*"– this with singular looks of alarm; and "...*how long 'she' planned on staying in Epping?*"– this last with definite looks of horror. The attack sent Susana into spasms of nervous laughter that did nothing if not fuel the women's skepticism and continue their barrage of questions.

Trying to hide her desire to turn around and flee, Cornelia spoke up, "We're just as much in the dark about the newcomer as you. We never set eyes on her before and frankly I wouldn't mind if we never did again!"

"She just came and sat herself down in the chair next to mine. She seemed like such a nice person– before the meeting, that is. I think she blew out my eardrum. She was a little on the loud side - wasn't she?" added Susana ineffectually.

Lynn Griggs, the village postmistress and owner of the village mini-market exclaimed, "Now that I think of it, I was probably the first person in the village to meet her. She came in and spent thirty minutes walking up and down the aisles checking out the shelves. I finally asked her if she needed any help and that's when she came up and introduced herself by saying she was lodging with Mrs. Brown. She didn't buy a thing, just asked me a lot of questions about the village and who lived where. If you ask me, she was snooping around and didn't care who knew it."

Unconvinced of the Leslies' innocence but with fresh material to sink their teeth into, the village women gathered around the postmistress, facilitating Cornelia and Susana's escape.

"Oh I'm so mad I could scream! That woman ruined my favorite meeting of the year. I could hardly pay attention to the proceedings because I was so mortified that everyone should think exactly what they *did* think! That woman - a friend of ours! I shudder just to think - don't you?" contemplated Susana as they made their way through the village towards Blandings.

As they approached the slight incline in the lane a sudden gust of wind sent the carpet of leaves swirling around their legs. Pulling her jacket tighter around her Cornelia chuckled and replied, "Don't you remember volunteering for the chili committee and the ballroom decorating committee?"

Susana made a vexed sound with her tongue.

"No, I don't. That woman made me so jumpy that I don't remember a thing about the meeting. Did I really volunteer for two committees?"

"Don't worry. I'm on the decorating committee so I'll cover for you if it gets too much for you. At least you didn't sign up for *every* committee the way Edith Kramer did."

"Well if you ask me, she had an uppity attitude and it's going to take me a long time to forget the looks on all the W.I. members' faces. I'm not at all sure she made a good impression. Are you?" said Susana reprovingly.

Before Cornelia could reply they were hit by a sudden gust of wind followed by fat raindrops.

"Ohhh dear, it wasn't supposed to start raining until tonight! We'll be soaked by the time we get home – do you have an umbrella in your purse?" cried Susana dully.

"Sorry, no umbrella. But it's a perfect excuse to go to the Tarts and Buns for lunch! C'mon, if we turn around and walk fast we can make it without getting too wet," said Cornelia, starting to walk fast while her sister did her best to keep up.

The Tarts and Buns Teashop was owned by Nora Clark, a native of Epping. She was not only a very talented pastry chef but also a good business woman incorporating a breakfast and lunch menu into her already famous pastry menu. This delighted the female population of Epping considering that for a vey long time the somewhat 'heavy' pub food at the Raven's Roost was the only option available.

Walking into the shop the sisters were astounded to see that every table was taken with W.I. members seeking refuge from the rain.

"Oh drat, now what do we do?" asked Susana pulling a tissue out of her purse and ineffectually wiping at her face and clothes. Almost immediately the sisters heard someone behind them calling their names. They turned around and saw a woman motioning to them to follow her while pointing to a table in a corner where another woman sat waving to them.

"You poor dears look like drowned rats!" laughed the woman. "We just made it in before the onslaught, you'd better join us or you'll never get seated."

"Debra, you're a life-saver! The rain is coming down harder than ever and we didn't even think to bring umbrellas. No one said anything about rain today and it was such a beautiful morning – do I really look as bad as all that?" replied Susana as they walked to the table.

"I'm chilled to the bone! I could use a nice hot cup of coffee. I was so rushed to get to the W.I. meeting that I didn't have time for breakfast. I'm famished!" asserted Cornelia.

Phyllis, the woman seated at the table stood up and greeted the sisters. "Hullo Leslies, haven't seen you in ages. All the excited chatter in here has to do with the Halloween Festival! We'd quite forgotten all about it...sorry Debra, hope you're not disappointed," expressed the woman seated at the table.

Debra O'Neil, author of children's books, was short and, owing to her fondness of Nora's pastries, a little on the plump side. Her cheerful personality was reflected in her fashion style that was mainly floral patterned dresses. Her fair, curly hair was cut in a short bob. Her habit of hiccupping whenever she felt nervous or agitated was a source of amusement for her friends.

Phyllis Stavis on the other hand was the polar opposite of Debra, her jolly disposition being the exception. She was a tall, big boned woman with short, dark hair and a no-nonsense attitude, which translated in a wardrobe of unflattering skirts, collared, long-sleeved shirts and jackets worn with laced shoes.

Phyllis held the position of superintendent of village schools with a doctorate in chemistry.

The women shared 'Larkspur Cottage', a charming nineteenth century house that they had lovingly restored. The cottage and its well-tended garden with larkspurs bordering the front lawn, was showplace in the village. Both were very well liked and respected and their monthly bridge party invitations were highly sought after.

Ginny and Liz, the two young servers, could be seen frantically scurrying from table to table trying to cope with the multitude of orders. Ginny approached the four women and wiping her forehead with the back of her hand she said, "Sorry about the wait, what with the end of the W.I. meeting and the rain we've had an onslaught of customers. You should see Nora in the kitchen, she's like an octopus with eight hands the way she's cooking and serving! Anyway, no time to stand here and chat, have you decided?"

Lunch at the Tarts and Buns Teashop was a prix fixe menu with a choice between two entrees, several salads and any pastry from the counter.

"You don't have to rush on our account, Ginny. We can see that it's a shark frenzy in here.

Hopefully you won't run out of food!" laughed Cornelia.

Phyllis chimed in, "Better order quickly then! Let's see, we have a choice of *Salmon Croquettes* and *Chicken Quiche*. Hmm, both delicious. I'll have the *Chicken Quiche*, please, and the *Tomato and Beet Salad*."

"It's a difficult choice, I love them both but I guess I'll go with the croquettes and leave some room for dessert. Oh, and I'll have a *Caprese Salad* to start please, Ginny," added Debra.

"Make that two, Ginny. It's always a treat when Nora has the croquettes on the menu," said Cornelia.

Susana, who always took several minutes deliberating, was typically last to order. "I've gone back and forth at least a dozen times but I suppose Debra's idea of leaving room for dessert is a good one so I'll also have the croquettes. But then Nora's quiches aren't at all heavy and the chicken quiche is my favorite. Drat, I can't decide. I know, I won't have any salad and I'll have one tiny slice of quiche and a couple of croquettes. I'm watching my weight – so frustrating, isn't it?"

"Now that lunch is settled I'm dying to find out what happened at the meeting. From all the jabbering going on here it must have been a humdinger of a meeting," observed Debra expectantly.

"Oh you should have been there! You've no idea the deaths by a thousand cuts I suffered!" ex- claimed Susana. "She sat right next to us when there were plenty of other seats available so of course everyone thought...OUCH! Cornelia, did you just kick..." Susana noticed that her companions were no longer looking at her. Instead, their eyes were raised and focused on something behind her. At the same time she sensed that the entire room had gotten suddenly quiet.

Before Susana could turn around she heard a familiar voice which nearly made her fall out of her chair. "Hey Leslies! I was wondering where everyone had gone to after the meeting! I just had a few things to explain to Petra and by the time I was finished you all had gone! I thought this was a sleepy little village but folks sure do move fast around here!"

At that moment, Ginny arrived at the table with their lunch.

"Hey are those fish cakes? Bet you've never tasted Louisiana crawfish. They make the best little cakes you've ever tasted. I guess American cooking beats English cooking every time!"

Ginny stood staring with round eyes and a gaping mouth while the four women stared at the speaker in confused astonishment.

Cornelia was the first to recover and with as much poise as she could muster replied, "As you can see we're just about to begin eating would you like to join us?"

Edith Kramer's shrill voice replied, "I'd love to! But not today, gotta go in to town on some business. How 'bout doing lunch at your place tomorrow?" And without waiting for a reply she turned around and made her way to the door, oblivious of the menacing stares.

"See what I mean? We're never going to see the last of her. I don't know why I started speaking to her. I could kick myself – do you really think she'll come over tomorrow?" groaned Susana.

"Probably," replied Phyllis. Then laughing added, "If she's the person you were telling us about I think we're in for one exciting Halloween!"

The next few minutes were spent giving Debra and Phyllis a description of Edith Kramer's performance at the W.I. meeting.

"Oh let's not let her ruin our Halloween. I'm going to see Madam Sonia today and it'll be my last costume fitting. So exciting! And no one ask me what it is because this year I'm keeping it a secret." Holding her fork up in the air and screwing up her face Susana continued, "I can't make up my mind which is more tasty. The croquettes have nice plump flakes of salmon and the fresh ginger is brilliant but the quiche could almost be a dessert with that delicious pastry. Isn't it wonderful?"

CHAPTER FIVE

After spending a satisfying couple of hours discussing the upcoming Halloween Festival the ladies walked out of the Tarts and Buns to a watery sunshine. Susana had been unable to resist stopping at the pastry counter and came out holding two pink pastry boxes, one of which she handed to Debra. "We only live once, and it's simply silly not to enjoy life - isn't it?" she said as the friends said their goodbyes.

Debra and Phyllis' cottage was located on a small cross street perpendicular to the village green just a few minutes walk from the Tarts and Buns. The center of Epping was situated in a meadow surround- ed by small hills and was known as 'the village'. Blandings had been built on one of these hills with a splendid view overlooking the village. As the Leslies walked toward the village green which would take them up the lane to their home, they saw their neighbor Sam Taylor driving down towards them. He was a handsome, middle-aged widower and it was said that after his wife's death he immersed himself in the running of his very successful dairy farm.

Pulling alongside them in his vintage 1975 Jeep, he greeted them amiably, "Afternoon Cornelia and Susana, hope you didn't get caught in the rain, it took people by surprise. Don't mind turning the car around and giving you a lift though," he continued in his clipped manner of speaking.

"We got soaked through and through on our way from the W.I. meeting but we made up for it with a very pleasant lunch at the Tarts and Buns. But I'm sure it didn't take you by surprise Sam – did it?" replied Susana, self-consciously patting her hair and almost dropping the box of pastries.

The handsome, weather beaten face retained a sparkle of the boyish good looks and the brown eyes that crinkled when he laughed continued to make hearts flutter. Sam Taylor was a respected leader in the community and held a seat as chairman of the selectman for the town. He maintained a polite and amicable relationship with the village residents and was a favorite at social events. However more than one well-meaning matchmaker learned the hard way that her effort to find him a wife was a waste of time.

Cornelia wondered at the timing of the farmer's drive down the hill and if it was purposely orchestrated when the bulk of the village ladies were safely back home or at work.

"The Women's Institute meeting this morning was a doozy. All the customary organization of committees with the usual suspects signing up for the various events, but it was taken to a new level by a newcomer, a Mrs. Edith Kramer. She had the entire hall in a silent uproar with Susana and myself in the middle," said Cornelia chattily.

"Ugh, she had me in a knot of nervous tension so much so that I couldn't concentrate on the meeting!

And Halloween is my favorite holiday. It's so disappointing because I always enjoy the planning – don't I?" grumbled Susana.

"I'm sure you'll be instrumental in making the festival a huge success as you do every year Susana.

By the way, don't forget that I'll be donating all the hay for the maze," replied Sam affably.

"Oh Sam you're such a dear! What would Epping do without you?" replied Susana.

"No need to thank me, happy to do it. But now I'm headed down to Hunter's Bosk as there's word the gypsies are in town along with some grumblings about them camping there. As chairman of the selectman I was asked to 'check things out' whatever that means. Maybe you'd like to come along?"

"We'd love to, thanks!" said Cornelia quickly opening the front passenger door and sliding in next to the farmer to the dismay of her sister.

Getting into the back seat and casting dark looks at Cornelia's back, Susana added, "Isn't the speed of the village telegraph astonishing? It hasn't been more than a couple of days since the gypsies made camp and already there's gossip and rumor. I think it's awfully exciting having them here so close to Halloween - aren't you?" She caught her breath suddenly and then in a quavering voice full of alarm said, "Wait a minute, we haven't been to Hunter's Bosk since that horrible accident last year, do we have to go?"

The tremor in Susana's voice alarmed her sister, "Well of course if you're not comfortable going I'm sure Sam won't mind dropping you off at Madame Sonia's since you already have an appointment there later today."

"Not a problem at all, and I'd be more than happy to pick you up on our way back," replied Sam.

Susana's dread of setting foot in Hunter's Bosk, if somewhat illogical, superseded her desire to be in Sam Taylor's company and she gladly agreed to the new plan.

CHAPTER SIX

Hunter's Bosk was a large forest on one side of Epping village. The land was protected and remained pristine with several species of oak some many hundreds of years old. Because the trees were primarily hardwood, the canopy was not overly dense allowing many types of flora to grow making it a favorite place for both avid hikers and more leisurely walkers. An old two-lane road bisected the woods and connected the center of the village to a more rural landscape composed of small farms.

After dropping off Susana at Madame Sonia's boutique, Sam and Cornelia set off for Hunter's Bosk.

"This is a real treat, Sam. I had intended to visit the gypsy camp when I learned they were in the Bosk," chatted Cornelia happily.

"Yeah, the way the 'village telegraph' operates nothing stays a secret for long around here," chuckled the farmer.

"Susana found out about it from Martha who dropped hints in her usual manner about finding *'lovely things'* from the gypsies and that she was going to win the costume contest. Apparently she's making her costume out of whatever she's bought from them, which frankly gave me the idea of coming to visit them myself. So I thank you for accelerating my shopping!" joked Cornelia.

"Glad to be of service, Cornelia. And now that you've brought up the Halloween Festival I was wondering if you wouldn't mind my escorting you to the Ball."

"Why I'd love it. Have you decided on a costume?" replied Cornelia somewhat stupefied.

"You know perfectly well that I don't wear costumes. But if you'd like, I could dress as a typical farmer," replied Sam with raised eyebrows and a lopsided grin.

Cornelia laughed and said, "Alright, I thought I'd give it a try. You actually look very smart in your dinner jacket so I'm not complaining. But I'll give you three guesses about what I'll be."

"Hmm, I really couldn't say," replied Sam making a good impression of thoughtful concentration. Then seeing the slight disappointment in Cornelia's face he quickly said, "Wait a minute, my guess is that you'll be either a gypsy or a witch."

"How did you guess?" laughed Cornelia with hidden satisfaction. "I'm trying to recall the last time we had gypsies camping in Epping. Do you remember they used to pass through every autumn when we were kids? The fun we girls had having our fortunes told! They were so full of excitement and romance," she continued wistfully.

The jeep ride was less than ten minutes and as they approached their destination the landscape of rolling hills and open farmland changed to forested countryside. The woods were enveloped in the light of early dusk when the farmer turned his jeep into a bisecting lane marked with a weather beaten wooden sign reading 'Hunter's Bosk'.

There was a cold, damp chill in the air as the two got out of the jeep. Cornelia tightened her scarf more securely and put on the gloves she kept in the pocket of her jacket. In the autumnal late afternoon light her attention was drawn to a plume of smoke.

"Look! That must be their camp!" she said pointing excitedly.

Making their way through the dark wood in the direction of the campfire, they could hear muffled laughter and singing. As they got closer the small glimmer of light that was left of the day gave way to a soft glow. Before actually arriving at the camp they saw stringed lights hanging from various trees adding to the festive atmosphere.

On reaching the gypsy camp and seeing the bevy of people engrossed in various tasks Cornelia could barely contain her enthusiasm and rushed forward to a dark, raven haired woman busy at work packing chestnuts into a container while a man beside her was operating the roaster.

"I hope we're not too late to buy a bag of chestnuts?" asked Cornelia breathlessly.

The woman looked up with huge black eyes that reflected the firelight and handing Cornelia a bag replied, "Not at all, we'll be busy here until late tonight."

Ever the gentleman, Sam pulled out his wallet before Cornelia could dig through her purse and handed the woman some change. The rest of the camp, seeing that there were paying customers, stopped the process of packing up and looked at the pair with expectant faces.

"Thanks Sam, have a chestnut and we can roam around looking at all their wares," said an animated Cornelia. She made her way to where an older man with a huge black mustache and a brown hat with a large crow feather stuck on the side was unfolding his wares. He smiled as Cornelia came to his stall piled high with vibrantly colored fabrics including shawls and scarves, all of varying size and material but all exquisitely beautiful.

"These are gorgeous! One is lovelier than the next!" exclaimed Cornelia. Then noticing that Sam was patiently at her side she gushed, "Aren't these splendid? Such wonderful workmanship!"

"Take your time, I have to find Yarko Ivanic in any case," replied Sam casually.

"You will not find any thing better than these anywhere, I guarantee. Gypsy-made is best in world and price is better," interjected the Gypsy in a thick accent. Then looking at the man in front of him with suspicion added, "Why you want Yarko?"

Not wanting any trouble, Sam introduced himself and replied politely, "Nothing to worry you, I'm a selectman in Epping village and was wondering how you're getting on here."

The gypsy's face grew sullen and he quickly motioned to an old woman whom Cornelia recognized as the gypsy fortune-teller. With wordless communication she nodded to him and took his place by the fabrics.

Perceiving an undertone of menace, Cornelia quickly murmured that it was late and they should be leaving. Turning, Sam replied, "Be right back. Go on with your shopping."

"Leave the menfolk alone, they know what they do, Cornelia," added the old woman in a kindly, quivering voice.

Taken aback by the woman addressing her by name, Cornelia replied haltingly, "You must be Zora the fortune teller. I'm sorry, it's been years since you've been in Epping and I didn't recognize you."

"You buy fabric. All pretty for costume. Halloween festival here soon. You tell Susana. She find many pretty things. Tell her she should not fear Hunter's Bosk."

Cornelia's mind raced trying to figure out how the old woman remembered them after all these years – not to mention knowing Susana's dread of the Bosk. In her nervous agitation she pulled out a large wad of money along with several scarves and shawls and handed them to the gypsy.

"You pay too much," said the gypsy shakily handing over the extra money. As Cornelia reached for the money the old woman held back her hand, stood up and pointed towards a small tent where a glimmering light emanated from the opening and added, "Better I read your fortune. Halloween will bring misfortune to the village of Epping."

Cornelia was relieved to see Sam approaching. Seeing several bags in Cornelia's hands he chuckled and asked if she had enjoyed herself.

Looking at her packages in bewilderment, Cornelia nodded assent. Grabbing Sam's arm she thanked the old gypsy woman and quickly lead her companion out of the woods leaving the gypsy with her change.

"I thought you wanted to hang around here?

Yarko told me there've been idle threats against them. Apparently some dolts have been harassing the gypsies not liking the fact that they've set up camp in the Bosk. I wish I knew the names of the idiots so I could give them a good thrashing."

Throwing her purchases into the boot of the car Cornelia grimly relayed Zora's warnings of the foreshadowed misfortune for the village.

"I hope Susana's not jumping up and down in a fit. You know how she loves her tea," said Cornelia anxiously.

CHAPTER SEVEN

Arriving at Madame Sonia's, Cornelia flew out of the jeep and entered the boutique only to find Susana and Madame Sonia seated by a tea table loaded with pastries.

Seeing her sister, Susana wiped her mouth and said, "Cornelia, you missed the most scrumptious tea!

I must have eaten at least a dozen cream puffs. Since she's almost next door to the Tarts and Buns Madame Sonia orders tea from them every day – isn't she lucky?"

Upon arriving at Blandings the sisters headed towards a delicious aroma coming from the direction of the kitchen. They were surprised to find Martha singing (bleating would be more to the point) at the kitchen stove.

Incredulous that the appetizing aroma could actually be coming from something Martha was cooking, Susana timidly asked, "Is that a new chili recipe? It smells heavenly – did Pinkey make it? That is...I mean...where's Pinkey?"

"Well, Ms. Nosey Parker, it's a new recipe but it's not chili. I worked on my chili this mornin' if you must know and I believe that I created the winnin' concoction."

"Concoction is right," murmured Cornelia under her breath.

That evening at dinner the Leslies sat at the dining room table in somber anticipation of Martha's ministrations. When Martha was left unattended to prepare a meal it was not uncommon for the Leslies to leave the dining room table with full blown indigestion.

Making it through a benign first course of sliced grapefruit the Leslies awaited the main course.

The moment of truth arrived when Martha walked in with a gravy boat that she placed with a thud on the table. "Darn, if I didn' forget the chops! They're so yummy Ms. Snooty there couldn't do any better," she said throwing a nod in Susana's direction. The sauce did indeed smell delicious and Jack, unable to stand the wait, took the ladle and placed a spoonful on his plate.

"Hey, this isn't at all bad. Let's hope whatever chops she made are half as good," said Jack relieved.

Knowing that she had everyone's attention, Martha walked in solemnly bearing the platter of lamb chops as if they were the crown jewels.

"What in the world does she have on her head?" whispered Cornelia as all eyes stared at the housekeeper.

A flamboyant headdress rivaling those worn by Carmen Miranda sat atop the housekeeper's red hair. She giggled coyly, and with seldom-seen shyness and the batting of her white eyelashes said, "I 'ad my fortune told today and a 'andsome man is comin' into my life. An' sure enough when I was at the butcher's the new assistanat was makin' eyes at me. He gave me a recipe for lamb chops. I think he called it 'Choked Cutlets'. I'm goin' back to the old gypsy woman tomorrow so's she can tell me when our weddin'll be."

Unable to take her eyes off Martha's headdress Susana whispered, "I think she means *'Smothered Cutlets'*".

"In case yur wonderin', I designed my chapow – that's French for hat - with scarves I bought from the gypsies today. Mitch, that's my feeahnsay's name, is gonna go gaga." Then setting the platter of scorched lamb chops next to the gravy boat she sniffed and said, "There's *some* that give compliments when they see beauty."

Knowing how to take a hint when they were hammered with one, the siblings laid it on thickly and then proceeded to serve themselves another one of Martha's gastronomic disasters.

"My advice is to *smother* the cutlets," said Jack as soon as Martha had left.

Thanks to Pinkey, the only member of the Jenkins family to inherit a complete set of gray cells, dinner had not been a complete loss. Before leaving early for a doctor's appointment she had made a huge batch of moist chocolate chip cookies. To the delight of her employers Pinkey enjoyed having Susana as her mentor. She was often seen delving into Susana's huge library of cookbooks to try out new recipes.

With dinner over Jack excused himself and went to his study, while Ann, Cornelia and Susana lingered over the cookies. Susana, taking the last bite of a cookie said, "It was all I could do to keep my mouth closed during dinner. I couldn't talk in front of Jack – you know how he is about gossip. And I couldn't say anything in front of Sam Taylor either. I've been biting my lips since we got home – are they bleeding?"

"Can whatever it is you're so desperate to tell us wait until we go upstairs? Actually I have something to tell you too," replied her sister.

"Uh oh, I was afraid of that. I told you not to go to Hunter's Bosk, it's probably haunted since 'you know what' happened there last year," said Susana fretfully. Suddenly putting up her hands in front of Cornelia's face she continued, "Wait, don't tell us until we go upstairs and I'm safely under the covers."

Ann laughed indulgently and said, "I'll have some Ovaltine with you but then I'm going to bed. I had to help clean out the stables today and I'm exhausted."

Settled in bed, Susana meticulously tucked the pink comforter all around her, fluffed up her pillows, and sank back with a sigh of pleasure which lasted two seconds before suspending her mug in mid air saying uneasily, "Alright go ahead with your horror story, I know I'm going to have nightmares - aren't I?"

Cornelia gave her an exasperated look, "No, silly. Hunter's Bosk is as peaceful as it's always been – or almost always. What I wanted to tell you is that Zora, you remember the gypsy fortuneteller from when we were kids? Well she's still at it. She must be in her eighties and..."

"See? I knew it! Something terrible is going to happen. That's what she told you, isn't it?" interjected Susana in a quavering voice.

Not wanting to cause her sister any more anxiety Cornelia had to think quickly. She decided not to tell her about the gypsy's dire prediction for the

Halloween festival. "Oh stop it, nothing terrible is going to happen, it's just that Zora surprised me by remembering both your and my name after all these years."

"That's all? She didn't gaze into her crystal ball and predict terrible destruction or..." Susana swallowed loudly, "more deaths?"

"I didn't have time to have a reading because we were in a hurry to get back in time to pick you up," said Cornelia crossing her fingers. "But an old gypsy named Yarko – who could have doubled for Bela Lugosi – told Sam that if the town didn't stop meddling in their affairs there was going to be trouble."

With perfect timing, an ominous rush of wind came howling down the chimney.

Susana slunk deeper under the covers and in a not very convincing attempt at liveliness said, "Madame Sonia told me the women of the village are driving her crazy with their insistence on total secrecy about their costumes while at the same time trying to wheedle information from her about everyone else's costume – I wonder if she can keep a secret?"

"Hm, the Masquerade Ball and Costume Contest are the best parts of the festival. Come to think of it, I'm also looking forward to the chili cook-off," said Ann.

"Thanks for reminding me! I met the food critic, Bruce Lingstrom in town today. Petra Aleman introduced us. He's very nice but in my opinion he looked a little too thin to be a food critic. Do you think he could have anorexia?" said Susana frowning.

"Wow, the Halloween Festival is making the big time," observed Cornelia.

"And guess who's giving Madame Sonia the hardest time? I'll give you three guesses - ready?" quizzed her sister.

Dramatically pausing to reflect Cornelia finally said, "You?"

"No, Miss Smarty Pants. Just for that you blew the other two chances. The award goes to Edith Kramer – big shock. Apparently she's in the boutique every day making changes and demanding that Madame Sonia assist her before anyone else. Madame Sonia said Edith's driving her towards a nervous breakdown – isn't it lucky that I already have mine done?"

"Doesn't surprise me in the least but I'm sure Madame Sonia can handle it. Oh, to answer your earlier question about the packages, I now have more than enough scarves of every size, color and description to last me at least four Halloweens," replied Cornelia repressing a yawn while heading for the door.

"Wait, don't forget that Edith invited herself to lunch tomorrow. What should we have?" asked Susana "Any cyanide in the house? See you in the morning," replied Cornelia as she and Ann closed the door behind them.

CHAPTER EIGHT

A thick layer of damp fog covered much of the countryside the next morning as Cornelia and Susana headed down to the village in the old Rover with the heat set at maximum. "I can barely see a thing in front of me. If I didn't know this lane by heart I'm sure we'd be in the ditch by now – wouldn't we?" reflected Susana.

"We could have walked, Susana. The rain has stopped and with the way you're driving it actually would have been faster and safer. If you don't speed up a little we're going to get to Lynn's after the meeting is over," replied her sister.

"Did you forget about Edith coming to lunch?

I don't know about you but I'd hate for anyone to see us with her. Thank heavens she's not part of the costume committee. She has half the women in town at the boiling point with her airs and affectation – aren't you dreading lunch?"

"I heard you telling Pinkey to make *Chicken Veloute* followed by a *Mushroom Omelette*. That's going to make for an awfully long time sitting at the table with her," replied Cornelia frowning. After a few seconds of contemplation, she continued, "I know, I'll call Pinkey and tell her to save the soup for dinner, forget the omelette and instead make a *Fresh Herb and Parmesan Risotto*! We'll serve tiny portions, eat quickly and get rid of her – tah dah!"

"What, no dessert?" asked Susana grimly.

"You can have your dessert *after* she's left," said Cornelia. Then looking at several cars parked in front of the postmistress' cottage said, "I knew we were going to be the last ones at the meeting."

Bluebird Cottage, the tiny house belonging to Andrew and Lynn Griggs, was, in typical country fashion, unlocked, and the sisters walked in without ringing. The pocket-sized entry hall was overflowing with umbrellas, gumboots and Wellies. Women's voices chattering happily could be heard quite close.

Being familiar with the cottage the Leslies entered another small room where a handful of women sat by the fire. As the Leslies entered, faces turned with words of greetings and two more chairs were brought out from the already depleted dining room.

With the last committee members settled comfortably with tea and biscuits, Lynn Griggs, the chairwoman of the costume committee commenced the meeting with an invitation for suggestions on various topics.

In a village the size of Epping, the dynamics between its female residents could generally be counted as mercurial. They could be beneficially adaptive or perversely inflexible depending on who they were up against or how the situation would influence their standing in the village. With the acumen typical of longtime village residents the women quietly assessed one another and, with what an outsider might regard as remarkable, came together in singular unity and the meeting progressed in friendly good humor. Suggestions from members received courteous acknowledgement and praise and this amicable and cheery attitude persisted until quite a bit had been accomplished.

Edith Kramer, who had been restlessly driving around the village in search of any kind of activity, drove passed Bluebird Cottage and noticed the cars parked in front. "Why not drop in and see what's happening in this deadbeat place?" she thought to herself.

She was dressed in leopard print tights and a faux fur jacket that was so 'faux' that it was colored bright purple. Getting out of her car her red stilettos sunk into an ankle deep puddle, making her scream with fury with a creative assemblage of four letter words. "No wonder the women here all look like death warmed over," she mumbled repeatedly shaking her left foot as she walked to the cottage.

The members of the costume committee were having a convivial time chattering away in great camaraderie and did not hear the front door opening.

It was only when Edith walked into the room that the animation suddenly and pointedly came to an end.

"Man it's cold out there and it's just October for heaven's sake! Are you all having some sort of meeting?" she asked the crowd of astonished faces as she edged her way to the fireplace.

As chairwoman of the committee it was left to Lynn to reply. "Hello Edith, we didn't see your name on the committee list. But in any case I think we're almost finished." With embarrassed side-long glances the rest of the women began to get up.

"Gosh gals, don't get up on my account. Have any of you been to the gypsy camp? I was just on my way home from there when I saw the cars out in front and thought I'd pass along some news."

Unable to resist the tempting tidbit (as Edith had guessed) the women stopped their ministrations and obediently sat down, still staring in apprehension.

Satisfied that she had the women's complete attention she continued, "That Zora's pretty good with her fortune telling. She told me some pretty fascinating things about Epping Village and between you and me, I don't think she pulled them out of her crystal ball. Now I know I'm just an outsider but I've seen how seriously you all take this here upcoming Halloween Festival so I'm gonna let you in on some inside info." The nervous rustling and looks of alarm fueled Edith's prattle. "It seems that the uppity seamstress is giving away details of costumes to anyone who walks into her shop," finished Edith highly gratified.

The looks of alarm suddenly changed to angry flashes as the women began casting suspicious looks at one another.

The momentary disquiet was broken by Andrew Griggs, Lynn's husband, who timidly put his head around the door and said, "Hate to interrupt you ladies' meetin' but the wind's startin' to kick up and it's goin' to get nasty soon." Having dutifully delivered the weather forecast he went back to the cozy kitchen to continue reading his paper.

The women, now sufficiently self-conscious but having been provided with a ready excuse to exit the meeting, bade each other hasty, feigned farewells, deaf to Lynn's forlorn voice announcing the close of the meeting.

Struggling with her Wellies, Susana silently prayed that Edith would not mention the upcoming lunch within earshot of the postmistress who was the only other person in the hall. Cornelia and the rest of the ladies were already outside quickly walking towards their cars.

Susana's worst fear materialized just as she managed to put one of her feet into a boot. "If I have to struggle into a pair of shoes they'd damn well better be haute couture or at least fashionable," observed Edith caustically.

"Yes...well...country living...lots of mud, isn't there?" replied Susana still struggling with her boots.

"You can say that again. Doesn't do much for style though, does it?" replied Edith, pointedly looking at Susana's outfit. As if a thought had just occurred to her she continued, "By the way, I'm not gonna be able to make lunch as I've got an important meeting. See ya."

Lynn, lips pursed in disapproval, turned and walked away, leaving Susana with the firm resolution to chuck the Wellies at her first opportunity.

CHAPTER NINE

Never one to hold to a schedule, especially one which involved work, Martha left Blandings directly after swilling down burnt coffee and headed for the butcher's. Normally, she would have assigned this job to her niece Pinkey, but in recent days Martha had been more than a little willing to take on this chore. While her employers were busy with their own engagements, Martha gamboled down the lane towards the village in her usual state of mindless preoccupation, with the one difference being that she actually was in a hurry to get to where she was going. With strength of purpose and much wrinkling of the forehead, she focused her mind (what little there was of it) on her destination.

By the time she arrived at the butcher's her multi-colored calf-length skirt was turned back to front, her blouse was partly untucked and, hardly ever bothering to put on a jacket in winter, the shawl she had tied around her shoulders was now hanging from her neck. Martha's short, curly, red hair which was perpetually in a state of frazzled chaos was trying its hardest to explode from it's confinement in a ponytail.

The village butcher shop was filled with customers eager to finish their shopping and get home before the weather changed. The village locals were well used to the eccentricities of the Jenkins family and fondly looked upon them with a sense of guardianship, so aside from smiles of greeting no one paid any particular attention to Martha as she jostled her way towards the front of the counter. Charlie Billers, who was the butcher and proprietor, was busy wrapping an order for a customer while politely answering another's questions. Noticing Martha shoving her way forward, he gave her a friendly greeting.

Martha wasn't paying attention. Her yellow eyes were focused on the other end of the counter.

She waived her bony arms in that direction and if that wasn't enough added a few *'you-hou's'* as well.

Mitch Harris, the new assistant and the object of Martha's attention was himself busy with an older lady who was having difficulty making up her mind whether to buy the pork roast or the pork loin. He was very patiently answering questions that only made the lady even more confused.

Unable to ignore Martha's ministrations or the amused faces of the other customers, Mitch quickly waived in reply and returned to address the indecisive lady.

"I'm goin' to give my order to you and no one else," giggled Martha batting her white eyelashes as she pushed a piece of paper across the counter, effectively settling the decision of the choice of meat for the ambivalent customer.

Mitch Harris had been at his new job for only a couple of weeks. Prior to that he had worked several years at the hardware store in the neighboring town of Milford. Cooking, which until recently had been something of a chore, had now become an obsession. Still only in his early thirties and having saved up some money he decided to learn the basics by apprenticing himself to various culinary trades. He had already spent a year working for a fishmonger and would spend another year working for Charlie Billers, learning as much as he could about the art of butchery.

In an effort to keep Martha's outrageous flirtations at bay, Mitch ignored her giggles and with a serious look, concentrated his attention on the piece of paper with her order. His face suddenly turning a deep red, he quickly put the paper in his pocket and in a somewhat higher voice than normal, told her that they could not fill her order due to the item being out of stock.

"What?" replied Martha. With more giggles and batting of lashes she said, "Silly, I didn't order nothin'! I was askin' if we was goin' to the movies tonight since I learned from good sources that yur gonna be my feeahnsay."

To Mitch's horror, the entire shop including Charlie Billers, were shamelessly taking in the spectacle and the only thing he could manage to say was a feeble, "Uh-huh."

CHAPTER TEN

After the disastrous morning at the costume committee meeting, Cornelia decided to calm her nerves by checking on her beloved rose garden to see if the huge project of winterizing the roses had begun.

With secateurs in hand she walked out of the potting shed which Bunter, the Blandings gardener, graciously allowed her to use. She had been meticulously pruning when she heard the crunching sounds of footsteps on gravel. Looking up she saw her sister heading her way in a (for her) unusually rapid pace.

A Deadly Prediction

"Cornelia, come quick! Reverend Peters is here asking to speak to us. He says that some distressing news has come to his attention and he wants to find out if we know anything about it – do we?"

"Oh for heaven's sake, Susana. How should I know if I haven't the faintest idea what you're talking about?" replied her sister in exasperation as she got to her feet.

"You're going to catch your death standing out here in this terrible weather. I just don't understand how you haven't caught pneumonia yet." Gazing up at the sky Susana continued, "Andrew Griggs was right.

With all those black clouds I'd say the nor'easter will be here any second now. Don't you think we'd better hurry to get inside?" As if in response, a distant clap of thunder sounded.

The Reverend Thomas Peters, a gentle and kindly man in his late seventies was the vicar of St. Mary's Church in the village of Epping. After receiving his undergraduate degree in theology at Oxford, he went on to pursue a post-graduate degree in philosophical religion, also at Oxford. He had been a quiet, studious young man, unpretentious and non-competitive, and although intrinsically shy, he had a quick wit, making him a favorite amongst his peers and at the local pubs in the college town. Upon completion of his studies his utilitarian character would not allow him to continue life as a scholar. He chose instead to make his living (like that of his father and grandfather) as vicar of St. Mary's parish, using his knowledge for the benefit of his parishioners. The parishioners could not have been more pleased and he quickly became a venerated fixture in their lives.

Entering the drawing room the sisters found the vicar quietly sitting in a chair with both hands resting on a cane held in front of him.

Protesting for him not to rise out of his chair the sisters quickly seated themselves wondering why he should come to Blandings without first phoning.

After politely asking about the progress of the Halloween Festival the vicar said, "I must tell you that Mrs. Hardy has been hinting of trouble brewing amongst the village women. Nothing much gets past my housekeeper, as you well know, and today I had visitors who gave me first hand information about animosity and manipulation in the committees. I do hope that everything goes smoothly with the preparations however I'm afraid that any more provocation could put the festival in danger of cancellation.

Thinking of Edith Kramer, Susana replied, "There's always a spiteful busybody who's always intruding in other people's business - isn't there?"

Then hastily blushing stammered, "Ohh…I'm so sorry…I hope I didn't offend you?"

The vicar's older sister had been the bane of the village. She never missing an opportunity to malign or ridicule and no one escaped her malicious gossip, which ultimately proved fatal.

"I take no offense, Susana. I'm fully to blame for my refusal to acknowledge certain things about my sister that caused the residents of this village so much pain. I failed not only my parishioners but the entire village and that will always be my burden," replied the vicar looking old and fragile.

Waiting until the vicar was safely home, Providence unleashed a torrential downpour, littering the roads with fallen branches. The unpaved roads became quagmires of mud and the lanes coming down from the surrounding hills turned into fast running rivulets. The driving was treacherous and was made at a snail's pace. If that wasn't enough, a power outage occurred just around the dinner hour.

At tea that afternoon it had occurred to the Leslie sisters to invite Sam Taylor along with Debra O'Neil and Phyllis Stavis for dinner in order to go over the vicar's concerns. As a fellow gourmet, Susana had graciously invited Bruce Lingstrom to join them.

If it had not been for the library's blazing fireplace, the Leslies and their guests would have been having cocktails and hors d'ouvres in complete darkness.

"Thank heavens Pinkey left before the storm hit. It didn't take us long at all to make tonight's dinner and the only thing Martha had to do was to put the food in the oven. That was ages ago so we won't have any problems - will..." Susana was interrupted by her brother who leaped from his chair and ran out of the room.

"Oh no," murmured Cornelia.

Jack returned and announced that dinner was laid out on the kitchen counter just as Pinkey had left it – uncooked and that Martha was nowhere to be found.

Suddenly, Jack found himself propelled into the room and in came Martha, wet hair clinging to her head and her soaked and drippping clothes accentuating her boney figure. Her feet made squelching sounds inside the gumboots that were covered in mud, leaving a trail of mucky patches behind her. With huge unseeing eyes she walked to the center of the library. The raging storm with periodic cracking of thunder and flashes of lightning which eerily lit up Martha's face added to the dramatic scene.

With a far off gaze and an affected, distant voice that would have brought envy to the heart of any thespian, Martha cried out, "*I come with a message from the Beyond...it brings warnings of misfortune. There is evil here that travels like a mist in the night bringing death in its wake.*"

Alright Martha, calm down, we're going to sit you by this fire and get your blood flowing before you come down with pneumonia," said Jack, taking her by the shoulders and guiding her to a chair which Sam had placed in front of the fire as the rest of the party gathered round.

With a look of concern Ann said, "From the looks of her she must have been in the storm an awfully long time."

"Yeah and she brought some of it back with her, "replied Phyllis staring at the mud soaked rug.

"Martha! Snap out of it! Why were you out walking in this storm?" asked an impatient Cornelia.

"Good luck getting an answer," murmured her brother.

"She'd win the costume contest in that getup hands down. Look at all that jewelry!" said Phyllis in admiration.

Forgetting her scare, Susana replied, "They're the latest fashion in jewelry - you know, the gypsy look?"

Having put Martha to bed with a sedative mixed in a glass of bourbon and milk, the Leslies and their guests decided to brave the elements and made their way down the hill to the Raven's Roost. Bert Colby, the proprietor, had installed a generator in the pub, which proved very valuable for both owner and customers. Stella, his wife, was a competent cook who could be counted on to have good English pub fare along with her interpretation of Italian classics known as the 'house specials'. However, the Leslies referred to them as *'Ketchup Italiano'*.

The eighteenth century building occupied by the Raven's Roost stood on a tiny side lane just off the main street of the village. It had originally been built as a small inn and pub but in the mid-twentieth century the owner had added modern conveniences, remodeling the inn into a comfortable home for his large family. Indoor plumbing and electricity were the only renovations made in the pub, leaving the low ceiling, oak paneled main room in its original state.

With years of smoke from both customers and the massive fireplace, the room, whose interior and bar counter were almost entirely paneled I oak, had acquired a dark, rich patina that was kept highly polished. The fire's reflection on all the surfaces gave off a warm glow, providing an invitingly snug respite from any weather discomforts.

Comfortably settled with drinks, the Leslie party politely looked over the evening's specials with everyone uniformly deciding on English fare. Almost at once Bert Colby was at the table and in his usual garrulous manner proudly described the evening's specials.

Susana, who had been thinking that the *Spicy Curry* would be aptly suitable on a chilly night, could not bring herself to injure the owner's pride and ordered the *Lasagna*. Debra, who was keenly sensitive to the feelings of others, enthusiastically ordered the *Chicken Parmesan* while the rest of the party remained steadfast, ordering a variety of typical pub fare, albeit somewhat self-consciously.

Bruce Lingstrom was a very good storyteller with an easy, down to earth manner and his dry wit gave his stories a humorous quality that was very entertaining. Dinner turned out to be an enjoyable evening filled with adventures in far off lands with foreign cuisines eaten in exotic places.

"Word is spreading that there's trouble with the gypsies camping in Hunter's Bosk. It's hard to believe some of the things some people are saying. After all it's not the first time that the gypsies have set up camp here in Epping," said Phyllis when Bert had left with their orders.

When Cornelia and I visited the camp Yarko, who seems to be the group's leader, told me that they've received threats. I couldn't blame him when he said that the gypsies would not stand for that type of treatment," remarked Sam.

With a worried look, Cornelia said, "It sounds like there's a lot of discontent going around. Reverend Peters told us today that he's very concerned about bickering and hostilities in the Halloween committees. Apparently people have gone to him to complain and he's worried that these squabbles might have a lasting impact."

Just then Bert Colby and a server approached the table carrying huge trays loaded with food.

Setting down the plates the beaming proprietor continued to stand by the table in eager anticipation of his customers' affirmation of his wife's cooking.

After receiving due praise and acknowledgement the good-natured Bert resumed his affected 'landlord' character and with jovial good humor looked around the room and said, "There's no end of talk about the village women being up in arms. I'm not complainin' as it's been good for business with all the menfolk comin' in more than usual just to get away from their wives' continual clamor about costumes and things.

Believe me, they come in here sick and tired of eatin' chili every night. Real cat fights in the village over chili recipes too. Just tonight I heard that even the vicar is gettin' involved on account of women going' to him to complain. It'd be a shame if all this hoopla spoils the Halloween Festival."

Bert Colby would have happily continued on this topic if it had not been for piercing laughter coming from just outside the pub doors. The customers turned inquisitive faces in the direction of the door. Seconds later a woman entered the room dressed in a full-length bright green gown, the ends of which were splattered with mud, and a fake white fox fur followed by a younger man dressed in jeans and a jacket. It was obvious that the young man was oblivious to his surroundings, his eyes focused solely on his female companion. Noticing that she was the center of attention and sweeping the room with a satisfied gaze, Edith Kramer's eyes rested on the Leslie table. With another ear splitting yell she greeted Susana and Cornelia, who by now were shrinking in their seats while their party looked on with raised eyebrows.

"No one told me we're supposed to be in mourning, 'cause it's as dead as a cemetery in here!" laughed Edith in response to Susana and Cornelia's rather doubtful greeting. Motioning to her friend she added, "Sorry we can't stay and party. We just stopped for a quick one 'cause Mitch here's gonna show me London's nightlife, aren't 'cha honey? Oh, by the way, that Zora out in those woods is a hoot!

Her crystal ball predicted ruin and misfortune at the Halloween Festival. And after all our hard work too!

But hey, why have a Halloween festival when it feels like Halloween here all year long?" The couple howled in laughter as they turned to leave. For almost a fully minute following this episode, the only sound heard was the pub sign swinging in the wind. Then as if on cue the room filled with murmuring voices.

"Where did you girls meet her?" asked a bewildered Jack.

Ignoring her brother Susana responded angrily, "I knew it, I just knew there was going to be trouble! Didn't I say *'doom and destruction'*?" With her usual flight of ideas she continued, "The man with Edith is the butcher's new assistant. Uh, oh, didn't Martha tell us he was her fiance?"

CHAPTER ELEVEN

Several days passed with the village engrossed in the final preparations for the Halloween Festival.

The Haunted Maze had been set up on the western field of Blandings, and the bleachers were set up on the village green ready and waiting for the Jack-O-Lanterns. The village women, along with some of the men, were all in a dither consumed with last minute costume adjustments, and Charlie Billers was doing a fine business with avid cooks frantically fine-tuning their chili recipes.

The morning prior to the start of the festival, Cornelia walked into the kitchen at Blandings to find Susana and Pinkey preparing breakfast.

"Good morning, everyone. You're here earlier than usual Pinkey, something important going on?" asked Cornelia.

"She was here before I got up. It seems that Martha was 'perfecting' her chili recipe all morning and called Pinkey for help. Isn't that right, Pinkey?"

"Not to help her with the cooking but to help, or rather, *do* all the cleanup. You should have seen the mess. Ketchup was everywhere! Oh darn, I missed a patch up on the ceiling," commented a frustrated Pinkey.

"Where is she now?" asked Cornelia somewhat guardedly.

"She's in her room fast asleep – I wonder how her chili turned out?" replied her sister.

"I have no idea. You wouldn't catch me tasting one of Auntie's originals. Did that once and never again. Hey, have you been to the gypsy camp yet? My boyfriend and I went last night and watched them dancing. The women are so beautiful with those gorgeous outfits and the music is amazing! There were several villagers walking around buying stuff and drinking the wine, really strong by the way. It was kinda funny to see the women going into Zora's tent. They'd first look around to see if anyone was watching and funnier still was when they came out looking mad as heck," volunteered Pinkey.

"Did you have your fortune told, Pinkey?" asked Susana.

"Oh sure, loads of times, but I'm not telling."

"Well I don't mind tellin'. And you know = what? It all come true! Last night my boyfriend aksed me to marry 'im – just like Zora said!" declared Martha with a self-satisfied grin and still in her Pajamas.

There was a shocked silence and then Susana and Cornelia spoke at the same time offering their best wishes.

"Tell us everything! That's so exciting Auntie!" exclaimed Pinkey enthusiastically.

With a deep sigh and a bored look, Martha babbled, "In the afternoon I went to have my fortune told, see? Last night Zora used some funny cards with weird lookin' pictures and told me that the stars were perfectly lined up in my astro-somethin' chart and it would be the best time for Mitch and me to get married. 'As anyone here made any coffee 'cause if not, I'm goin' back to bed."

"Was Mitch there with you?" asked Susana.

Giving her employer a pitiful look, Martha said, "My, my, aren't you the nosey one? 'e had to work last night but I went to Charlie's and told my feeahnsay that I was goin' to wait for 'im so's we could go to the vicar's."

"*You're married?*" asked Susana in shock.

"Listen, Ms. Nosey Parker, I'm only gonna say this once. We didn't see the vicar 'cause Mitch had an important meetin' to go to but we're officially engaged and gettin' married tonight. Okay?" She then flashed a withering look at her audience and with great dignity proceeded to bump her way back to her room.

"That Mitch sounds like a player, doesn't he?" declared an astonished Susana.

For the next few days the weather was unseasonably mild with the forecast calling for much of the same through the Halloween Festival. However, in lieu of celestial tempests the village of Epping was destined for storms of a different kind.

The sisters spent the morning at diverse tasks.

Cornelia, taking advantage of the fine weather, prepared her roses for a winter onslaught while Susana was in the kitchen contentedly baking *Madeleines* for the afternoon tea. It had been decided that directly after lunch they would go into the village to do some last minute shopping before the festival.

Expecting to pick up her costume from Madame Sonia's and impressing upon her sister that there would be quite a few shopping bags to carry, Susana succeeded in convincing Cornelia the necessity of motoring into the village.

Five minutes later she was being dropped off at the fashionable boutique with Cornelia heading for

Hunter's Bosk. She was intent on finding out if Zora was at the root of the village discontentment.

Parking the car at the edge of Hunter's Bosk, Cornelia followed a path leading to a small clearing where the gypsies had set up their camp. The sound of men's voices raised in anger stopped her in her tracks. As she was still a good distance from the encampment she realized the voices could not be coming from there. However they seemed to bounce off the hardwood trees making it difficult to pinpoint their direction. Not wanting the embarrassment of running headlong into an argument, Cornelia strained her ears trying to decipher the direction of the voices that continued in bitter dispute. At one point she thought she recognized one of the voices but then the other rallied back and the familiarity vanished. Shortly after, the voices stopped, leaving only the familiar sound of birdsong high above her. Shrugging her shoulders she continued towards the gypsy camp concentrating on the questions she would ask Zora. Coming around a particularly thick growth of trees she stopped abruptly just before running into a man similarly deep in thought. Attempting to regain her composure after her bad fright, Cornelia stammered an apology only to be exasperatingly waived off with an angry growl as he stormed past her towards the edge of the woods.

Stumbling into a clearing Cornelia once again came close to a collision but this time with a group of hens dementedly running around in the spongy moss of Hunter's Bosk, Cornelia noticed that the gypsies were just starting to put out their wares for that evening's sale. Turning to walk to the fortune-teller's tent, she was surprised to see Zora sitting by the fire watching her.

"I was just thinking how strange it is to not see any visitors, you usually have dozens of people here. Has anything happened?" asked Cornelia somewhat hesitantly.

Ignoring Cornelia's question and turning to walk to her tent, the Gypsy woman said, "Come, I will read your fortune. I have been expecting you."

Caught unawares and feeling powerless to object, Cornelia followed the Gypsy into the purple and green tent. Inside it was just as she remembered. The entire vertical space was covered in richly pleated midnight blue velvet curtains with the ceiling draped in black velvet with subtle twinkling lights that very effectively represented a midnight sky. The furnishings consisted of a round table covered in a deep purple velvet cloth, two chairs, one already occupied by Zora, and a small table next to the gypsy containing all the implements necessary to fortune-telling, including a very ordinary looking crystal ball. Candles flickering in standing wrought- iron holders in each of the four corners set the mood.

Resigned to her fate, Cornelia sat opposite the gypsy and silently waited for her to begin. The elderly gypsy's thin appearance was exaggerated by her preference for wearing black with the exception of a brightly colored flowered shawl. Her jet black eyes reflected the candlelight and Cornelia thought them more kindly than menacing.

Folding brown, claw-like hands on top of the table, the gypsy spoke solemnly, "I will not keep you long nor will I use the aid of any devices as I know the reason for your coming here today. I will tell you that yes, there is mischief in the village of Epping and that it will continue its path without anyone being able to counter the effects. Know that it is not gypsies who are at the cause of this evil. The harm has already taken root and it will culminate at your festival."

Too shaken to respond, Cornelia sat ineffectively staring at Zora. Getting her wits about her she tried to formulate a coherent response but was prevented from so doing by loud voices coming from outside.

Sliding back the velvet curtain covering the entrance, Zora looked at Cornelia and said, "Go now."

Unsure of what just happened, Cornelia walked out as if in a fog, not noticing that the camp was now filling with people. She walked past a group sitting by the fire drinking wine and speaking in low tones. She felt very cold and the warm fire and wine looked very inviting. Suddenly she felt a tug at her jacket and Edith Kramer's shrill laughter.

"Well fancy seeing you here! Did ya have your fortune told? That Zora's a gas isn't she?"

Startled, Cornelia looked to see not only Edith, who was more than a little wasted, sat alongside Mitch Harris, Yarko and the stranger with whom she had almost collided. The three men glanced up with menacing looks, obviously not happy at having been interrupted, and without speaking glared at Cornelia. Her arms around Mitch and impervious to the men's mood or too drunk to care, Edith invited Cornelia to join them. However Cornelia was saved the embarrassment of a reply by something whizzing past her head, hitting a tree and shattering behind her. Almost as quickly a figure lunged itself into the group of men and with flailing arms and legs kicked and punched Mitch Harris.

Cornelia immediately recognized the long, spindly limbs and flashes of red hair and rather stupidly tried to grab at them while Edith stood watching in spasms of laughter. Yarko, who was by far the most muscular of the men, was finally able to suppress Martha although her ear-splitting screams and protests continued. Zora, who had been quietly watching this chain of events, walked up to Martha and with a slap across her face stopped her hysterics.

With unsteady hands, Cornelia took hold of Martha and walked her to the car, silently hoping that Martha's frenzy would not recur. Thankfully, her fears were unwarranted as once in the car Martha's mood did an about-face and with a self-satisfied, looney chuckle, she said, "I showed that lout he can't cheat on me!" And with that she put her head back and promptly fell asleep.

As she drove to the village center with her head pounding, Cornelia tried to sort out the afternoon's events but they were all running together in one big jumble. Her thoughts were interrupted when she heard Martha mumbling in her sleep. Quickly glancing at her passenger, she was reassured that Martha was still fast asleep despite an evil grin on her face. "Knowing Martha she'll forget the whole thing by dinnertime," thought Cornelia optimistically.

Pulling up to Madame Sonia's, Cornelia spotted her sister just coming out of the boutique. A large wardrobe bag draped over one arm and holding several shopping bags in the other.

Susana shuffled her way to the passenger side 0f the car, but when she saw a mass of red hair leaning against the window she gave Cornelia a quizzical look and then heaved herself and her packages into the back seat saying, "Don't bother to tell me because I don't want to know – is she alive?"

"'Course I'm alive you ninny, I've just been puttin' my brain to work on how to kill that snivelin' Mitch and the witch that was all over 'im," countered the housekeeper, making both sisters sit up in alarm.

CHAPTER TWELVE

Arriving at Blandings with their ditzy housekeeper in tow, the Leslie sisters watched in wonder as she dashed to the kitchen and began a flurry of banging and clanging as she pulled out pots and pans in willy-nilly fashion.

"Do you think she's going to use those as weapons?" whispered Susana a little too loudly in an effort to be heard over the din.

"No I ain't gonna use my pots," replied Martha, mocking Susana's voice. In her voice added, "I'm makin' my chili for tomorrow's contest. That no good Mitch 'arris ain't the only one who can make chili.

Don't you two 'ave anythin' better to do than mindin' other people's business?"

In true Leslie fashion, the sisters backed away from their housekeeper in search of safer quarters.

"Thank goodness we got away! I was afraid she'd ask us to stay and taste her chili. You won't believe the things Madame Sonia told me today! Oh, and I saw Petra and Lynn who were also picking up their costumes. Do you remember at the last Halloween Ball committee meeting Edith Kramer volunteered to take care of all the arrangements with the party rental company? Well Petra Aleman went to the Hall this morning and it was completely bare and when she called the rental company they hadn't received any calls regarding the festival. They felt badly about the situation and agreed to send out all the necessary things but couldn't provide the people to do the set up because they were working a wedding in Concord. The committee members are expected to be at the hall this afternoon to get everything set up. And if that's not enough, you and I have made the persona non grata list because everyone's convinced we're best friends with Edith," said Susana gloomily. Then in an even gloomier tone she added, "Do you think Martha's going to serve us her chili for dinner?"

Entering the town hall the sisters received a chilly reception from their fellow W.I. members who held them responsible, albeit unjustly, for Edith's failure to follow through on her offer, thereby forcing them to work on the eve of the festival. The women worked through the afternoon and into early evening arranging tables and chairs, setting up buffet tables, laying down tablecloths, napkins, and placing dinnerware and crystal in their proper places. By the time all the Halloween decorations had been placed on the tables with the Halloween lanterns strategically set up for the best effect and the Hall stage festively decorated for the costume contest, it was almost the dinner hour and the women were becoming increasingly irritable. With the last decoration in place the harried women dashed off to their homes to make finishing touches on costumes and last minute additions to their chili recipes.

Cornelia and Susana arrived home in a state of exhaustion with Susana in a grumpy mood over having missed her tea. Entering the kitchen they were surprised to find Pinkey taking out a roasting pan from the oven with a delicious aroma of garlic and chicken.

"Oh Pinkey, you're wonderful! The chicken smells and looks heavenly! But you're not supposed to be here after dark! Is anything wrong?" exclaimed Susana who had been contemplating feigning an illness if Martha were to serve her chili for dinner.

Beaming, Pinkey replied, "Thanks Mrs. S., I heard that the decorating committee had to stay late and do the set up at the Hall and since Auntie was hogging the kitchen all afternoon with her chili I figured you wouldn't have time to cook, so after Auntie finished I decided to surprise you by making that chicken recipe I saw you make one time. I think you called it, '*My Son Chicken*'."

Coming home from their respective offices in the City, Jack and Ann rushed to the dining room just in time to enjoy the '*Maison Chicken*'. Pinkey's efforts did not go without considerable compliments and left the room blushing with satisfaction. For several minutes the only sound in the room was silverware against china as the family enthusiastically savored the meal.

Looking up from his plate, Jack wondered out loud, saying, "The chicken is delicious but how come you two are so quiet? Frankly I'm surprised that you aren't in your usual flurry of excitement with last minute preparations for Halloween."

The sisters looked at each other in sad contemplation of their brother's lack of observation.

With a deep sigh Susana volunteered, "If it weren't for the fact that Pinkey went out of her way to cook tonight I'd be in bed nursing a headache. I'm completely exhausted. Aren't you Cornelia?"

Responding in the affirmative Cornelia explained about their unexpected labors at the hall, "And that was after spending the early part of the afternoon at

Hunter's Bosk, which I swear was filled with raving lunatics – one of whom was Martha… wait, that's no surprise. I had to literally pry her off of Mitch Harris, the butcher's new assistant."

"You actually broke up a passionate embrace?" asked Ann giggling.

"Passionate is right, she was trying to scratch his eyes out! Not to mention that she almost brained me with a bottle that was intended for the poor guy," replied Cornelia critically.

"There, you see? I told you Hunter's Bosk was haunted, didn't I?" remarked her sister with mild indignation. But in true character the next minute she was out of her chair and off to the kitchen to get dessert.

"I didn't want to say anything in front of Susana but I was actually spooked by Zora the old gypsy woman today. She's caught me off-guard twice now with her prescience *and* she said there's evil in Epping and something about it coming to a head at the festival."

"Great, now you're believing all this hocus-pocus stuff. Are you sure it's not your imagination taking over so close to Halloween?" replied her brother.

Just as Cornelia was about to respond Susana came in with a tray of *Panna Cotta* which completely took their minds off the day's labors and they happily reminisced about past Halloweens.

After the last bite of dessert was eaten, Ann noticed her sisters-in-law's drooping eyelids and stifled yawns and kindly offered to do the clearing up on her own, suggesting that Cornelia and Susana head on up to their beds, which they gratefully accepted.

On the way up the stairs, Susana suddenly stopped and said, "I just remembered what I wanted to tell you! Sorry, my headache must have driven it out of my mind. Let's go back and get some Ovaltine and a little more dessert, okay?"

Thankfully climbing into her bed, Susana sighed with contentment as she took a bite of *Madeleines* leftover from tea and sat back against the pillows and dreamily looked at the wardrobe bag containing her costume while she waited for her sister.

With a renewed burst of energy, Cornelia took little time to wash up and get into her pajamas. Settling herself in the divan she remarked, "Boy did we have a strange day. We could make a movie out of this Halloween – we certainly have the perfect characters. The only thing we're missing is a..."

Susana raised her hand in a motion for her sister to stop, "Don't say it! You were going to say the 'M' word, weren't you?"

Unable to rid herself of Zora's foreboding predictions but not wanting to alarm Susana, Cornelia responded, "Don't be silly, I'm only joking. I guess Jack's right, my imagination is on overdrive."

In an unusual reversal of roles, Susana reassured her sister. "It's perfectly understandable when it's Halloween and we have the Kramer in our midst acting like a witch. Madame Sonia is convinced she's the one that's spreading the rumors about giving away everyone's costume designs. And according to Lynn and Petra, Martha's been spreading the news of her engagement all over the village. I just can't see her married - can you?" Susana sunk deeper into her pillows in happy anticipation of her favorite holiday.

Pleading exhaustion, a worthless endeavor as Susana was already sound asleep, Cornelia went to her room where she spent a fitful night dreaming of gypsies whirling madly around a blazing campfire.

CHAPTER THIRTEEN

On the morning of the Halloween festival Mother Nature stubbornly refused to follow the weather forecastors' instructions and she painted the dawn sky with red streaks, signaling a storm.

As people who live in the country know, whenever there's any type of public celebration the village children are the first to congregate noisily on the green. On this morning the village center was already in a flurry of activity with everyone eagerly awaiting the official opening of the festivities. This honor had long been held by Lady Millicent Gaspari, an octogenarian who had the misfortune of resembling a fat bulldog. She was the daughter of an earl and the widow of a charming Italian gigolo who for years had happily gone through her inheritance until there was nothing left and then with clockwork accuracy, succumbed to a fatal heart attack leaving his wife as poor as the proverbial English church mouse, Lady Millicent survived on a tiny pension that allowed her to live in a small cottage in the village with a companion/housekeeper whom she continually pestered. She had a regular routine of strolling along the village green while barking instructions to her hapless companion.

In her excitement Susana had slept very little and awakened well before dawn to prepare breakfast.

When the rest of the family came down sniffing appreciatively at the aroma of fresh brewed coffee, she was setting down a pitcher of maple syrup in front of steaming pancakes. As they sat to enjoy their breakfast they jabbered excitedly about their various plans at the festival while making self-conscious banter about their costumes.

In keeping with English country tradition, the festival was formally opened with loud fanfare. The labyrinthine haunted maze that had been elaborately laid out by Sam Taylor with the help of the town firemen already had a long line of people waiting at the entrance. With the official opening several dozen more rushed to get in line for the privilege of being terrified by the zombies and demons that were enthusiastically portrayed by the spirited firemen.

By mid-afternoon tickets for the chili cook-off had sold out and the venue was in full swing with hungry people lining up to taste the many entries. The village was beginning to fill with people who had had the foresight to bring along blankets. Ardent cooks eagerly served helpings of their guarded recipes, eyeing their competitors suspiciously. With the Raven's Roost closed for the occasion, several men escaped to Bert Colby's beer kiosk. In preparation for the judging later that day, Bruce Lingstrom, the much touted food writer was happily rooted in a chair already partaking of the preferred beverage.

With dusk approaching the spooky atmosphere heightened and the village green was alight with hundreds of uniquely carved Jack-O-Lanterns festively flickering in the moonlight, casting strange, goulish shadows.

By nine o'clock in the evening the only sounds on the village green were the voices of a handful of teens. The adults were busily donning costumes in preparation for the much-awaited Masquerade Ball.

Blandings Manor was the scene of uproarious laughter as each costume was appraised and reviewed as the Leslies and their guests, Sam Taylor and Bruce Lingstrom sipped cocktails in the library.

No one was immune from the good-humored critiques.

A limo had been hired for the occasion and it was with a great deal of pushing and jostling of costumes that the partygoers managed to finally get into the car.

"This crown just doesn't want to stay on my head - is it tilting?" asked Susana while fluffing out her gown's enormous folds of lavender tulle, which were already covering Jack and the food critic who sat on either side of her.

"Yes, Glinda, Good Witch of the North, it's at a very jaunty angle but at the risk of sounding like a bore, would you please keep your scepter from piercing my eye?" replied her brother.

"So sorry, Sir Robin, but my gown gets in the way. It's like a bubble bath gone out of control - funny isn't it?" responded Susana with as much dignity as possible.

By the time the Leslie party came down the lane to the village, the Masquerade Ball was in full progress and they could hear loud laughter and music coming from the Hall.

"Oh dear, I hope we're not the last ones to arrive. Don' you hate making a grand entrance?" said Susana in an excited voice while fussing with her hair and gown. The party was definitely in full swing with merrymakers already more than a little tipsy while others spilled into the vestibule from the crowded dance floor. The noise was at a cacophonous state with everyone competing with the music in an effort to be heard.

"Isn't it funny how people become completely uninhibited when wearing costumes?" whispered Jack in his wife's ear as the group squeezed their way into the main ballroom.

Without looking at Jack, Ann whispered, "We must look funnier than everyone else because people are staring."

Trying to make her way to the table Susana said, "Everyone's stepping on the hem of this idiotic gown. It'll be a miracle if it makes it to the table in one piece – is my backside still covered?"

Cornelia and Sam had decided not to continue the struggle to the table and instead joined in the dancing. Just when she was starting to enjoy herself Cornelia felt eyes boring into her back and then a couple wearing masks came along side of them and a woman's slurred speech could be heard, "Edith told us you were going to be in a stripper's outfit! 'Gor that would 'a been hilarious!"

"Let's head over to the bar. You won't believe how much of a better dancer I become after only one drink," laughed Sam in an effort to save Cornelia embarrassment. The rest of the party had valiantly made it to their table where Debra O'Neil, Phyllis

Stavis, Chief Constable Major Geoffrey Sandowne and Mrs. Sandowne were already seated.

"Is it me or have you noticed that people are staring at us?" asked Susana.

"To put it succinctly, we did. Someone in a mask told me that Edith was telling people I was going to be wearing a stripper's costume," replied her sister as she and Sam sat down.

"Yeah, they blame you girls for being her friends and the reason she's in Epping," added Debra.

"I guess that solves the mystery of the weird stares," said Sam with a grin.

"Mmm, this poached salmon with the curry cucumber sauce is excellent! Anybody want a bite?" offered Susana making her way from one of the buffet tables.

"Speaking of curry, I spent some time today discussing what makes a good curry. Is it the spices or the meat? In my opinion it's the spices," volunteered the food writer.

A lively dialogue ensued as to the various merits of each but before a consensus was reached Mitch Harris approached the table holding a martini glass whose contents were quickly spilling onto the floor. His free hand grabbed hold of the table for support while the last dregs of the martini fell on the tablecloth. Slurring his words he asked if anyone had seen Edith. Not receiving the answer he wanted he curled his lip and swayed in a collision course towards the other tables.

"I knew something was strange. We haven't heard any loud boasting since we got here," observed Cornelia matter-of-factly.

Her brother frowned and said "Funny, the Jenkins family are sitting together but I don't think I've seen or heard Martha all night. I'll go over and ask them if they know where she is."

Jack's troubles proved fruitless. On his way back to the table the lights were turned out and Petra Aleman appeared in a spotlight in the center of the dance floor asking if Bruce Lingstrom would step up to announce the winner of the chili cook-off. The room became instantly quiet with anticipation.

After a brief yet gracious speech praising all the entries and acknowledging the aptitude of the cooks, the food writer announced the winner of the contest. To the amazement and revulsion of the audience, Edith Kramer's name was pronounced the winner.

Just as the room had become suddenly silent it just as suddenly exploded in a buzz of angry voices.

"At the W.I. meeting she said she wasn't going to enter the contest!" shouted a female.

"I bet she sabotaged the other entries!" came another voice.

Bruce Lingstrom stood red-faced and tongue-tied in complete bewilderment of the situation.

Fortunately for him, Petra Aleman grabbed the microphone and called for the lights and music. As the people in charge of operations were either inflamed members of the W.I., their husbands and/or village residents, her request was ignored.

In perfect synchronicity a low moaning was heard sending the already overwrought revelers in one seemingly choreographed movement to turn towards the sound. The room was now in almost total darkness, making it impossible to see anything and increasing the angst. Slowly, a floating white face, it's body camouflaged in the dark, appeared. At first a few chuckles were heard from people thinking it was part of the program. But when the face began to speak everyone stood silent and frozen in place.

"'*Zora sees Death, Zora sees Murder. The stars have spoken yet you have not listened. Now it is too late. Zora can no longer help.*'"

Just as quickly the face vanished and a loud thud was heard. Almost at once the vestibule doors swung open and Billy Jenkins, the Epping Village constable, crashed in yelling for the Chief Constable while tripping over a body that was slumped exactly where the face had been. This time the lights were hastily turned back on.

CHAPTER FOURTEEN

The eerie silence was broken by the labored breathing of the pudgy constable forcing his way through a crowd that had remained frozen in place by the bizarre string of events. Already more than a little winded the constable's full lips systematically opened and shut in an effort to breathe, his protuberant eyes were now double their normal size and his red face was drenched in perspiration. All in all he resembled a fat carp flailing out of water, propelling himself, if somewhat clumsily, towards Major Sandowne who had come forward to meet him. The constable gasped, "Dead...in pond...wedged...branch."

The natural curiosity of the villagers forced them to gather round the constable but his cryptic message was now the proverbial straw on the camel's back. Amidst shrieks citing the 'Curse of the Gypsies', at least a couple of women fell in dead faints, with the rest continuing their howling of the fulfillment of gypsy predictions.

After a few moments of huffing and puffing the constable was able to form a somewhat coherent explanation of the situation. This amounted to a female body having been found in the Epping village pond by a group of teenagers who were now waiting in a room just outside of the ballroom. The body was definitely female but it could not be identified because it was face down in the water. The teens had called the police station and the officer in charge, an elderly and sardonic man by the name of Dibbs was forced, much to his regret, to send Jenkins and another constable to the scene.

"Shall I go speak to the witnesses, Chief Constable?" asked a male voice in a Mummy costume.

Turning to the familiar voice struggling to remove bandages, the C.C. said, "Rogers! Splendid good luck to see you!"

"Isn't our Halloween the best?" gushed Susana delightedly. Hearing her brother's groan she self-consciously continued, " I didn't mean NOW, I meant...oh I don't know what I meant - do you?"

The C.C. continued in a self-conscious attempt to regain control and he addressed the young man. "Ahem...splendid good luck to have you. Yes, we'll need to get the young peoples' statements."

Sergeant Michael Rogers of the C.I.D. New Scotland Yard was a native son of Epping Village. He had been on the force for a little over four years and while he lived in the City he considered Epping Village his true home and visited on a regular basis. Sergeant Rogers, followed by Constable Jenkins, made his way to the room where the teens were waiting. The group of five obviously scared and shaken teens looked up with frightened faces as the policemen entered the room. None of them spoke a word hoping that they wouldn't be asked to describe what they had found. Still on the right side of thirty, Sergeant Rogers spoke to them with an effort to sound as little like a police officer as possible. Almost at once the teens began to feel more at ease and the interviews progressed without mishap.

"Not much they could tell," explained Rogers to the C.C. "Seems they were taking the path along the pond as a shortcut to the cemetery until one of their flashlights lit up what they thought was some clothes caught up in a fallen tree. On closer inspection their worst Halloween nightmare came true," related the Sergeant.

"Alright so no one can identify the body because she's face down. You understand that we don't have the manpower to conduct a proper investigation of this sort. I'll leave it to you to call in your people. I'll expect you and your crew at the station tonight. Constable Morris will stand guard at the pond until they arrive and Jenkins is taking down the names of every person here. Hard to believe we're going through this again," said the Chief Constable shaking his head.

"Well girls, I hope you're satisfied with this year's Halloween festival," said Jack with a crooked grin as they walked into Blandings.

"We couldn't have dreamed of a spookier one, that's for sure," countered Cornelia.

"I don't know whether to be excited or frightened to death. It's positively uncanny how this Halloween has turned out. Do you think anything else will happen?" asked Susana shakily.

"You sound just like one of the villagers with their silly superstitions. Next you'll be saying that Zora put a hex on the village," remarked her sister.

It was in the wee hours of Halloween morning that Constable Dibbs placed a tray with steaming mugs of coffee and sandwiches on the Chief Constable's desk. Across from the C.C. were Chief Detective Inspector Alistair Bunson of New Scotland Yard and Sergeant Michael Rogers.

"Might as well sit back and enjoy the hot coffee while we wait for Doc Goodman's report," said the C.C.

"In all my years growing up in Epping we never had *one* murder let alone two. I mean this is Epping, not London!" observed the Sergeant with feeling.

"That's as may be but it's *people* who commit murders not villages, cities or any one place. And with last year's experience I've come to realize that a small community can harbor all sorts of resentment that only fester with time. The difference is that villagers are too wrapped up in each other's lives to notice any peculiarities. And if they do notice them they're just ignored 'cause they're too close to home, literally *and* figuratively. But I understand what Michael here is saying. It's just not like this village to have this kind of thing happen all over again. We're just getting over the last incident." replied the C.C. with some emotion.

With a knock on the door Constable Dibbs entered with the autopsy report. Taking a few moments to read the document the C.C. looked up and with a resigned sigh said, "'*Cause of death at this time is undetermined. Body immersed in water for not more than two hours. Further tests by the Scotland Yard forensic laboratory will be done to determine if the death is or is not consistent with drowning.*' I'll contact the county coroner and suggest that he set the inquest for later this afternoon."

CHAPTER FIFTEEN

"So the case is wide open, which nine times out of ten means a homicide. You only have a few hours to speak to everyone who knew her," said Inspector Bunson to his Sergeant.

"That's going to be difficult, Inspector. From the information that Mitch Harris gave us, that's the person who identified her, she'd just moved into Mrs. Brown's lodgings about two weeks ago," replied Sergeant Rogers.

"Oh lovely, not only am I going to have to deal with hostile villagers but now they have the added advantage of ignorance as well," observed Inspector Bunson.

"Not quite Inspector, a few of the villagers told me that the Mrs. Leslies were great friends of the deceased," replied the Sergeant hopefully.

"Those two sisters? *Again*? Now where did I put those tablets?" exclaimed the Inspector fumbling in his coat pocket for his antacids.

Inspector Bunson was a highly respected and well-liked veteran of Scotland Yard. A hang-dog personality and chronic indigestion gave those who didn't know him the impression of incompetence mixed with a lack of ambition. In reality he had a facile mind and the methodology of his investigations were characterized by meticulous persistence. Seemingly innocuous words, actions or gestures would stick in his mind to be pulled out and ruminated over at a later time. He had a habit of twitching his nose and mustache whenever he was in one of these moods and his colleagues had learned long ago the folly of interrupting his thoughts. For this reason he had been nicknamed 'Bunny' – but never to his face.

During the very early hours a northerly wind began to howl through the leafless trees. At eight o'clock in the morning, under a dark, slate colored sky and with only a few hours of sleep the Inspector and his Sergeant pulled up to the Tarts and Buns for breakfast. With not much to go on, Inspector Bunson decided to visit Mitch Harris and Mrs. Brown, the two people who had ties with the dead woman.

"I'm starving! I don't know why but whenever I'm in Epping my appetite increases. It's probably that food just tastes better in the country," observed Rogers, fighting against the wind to hold the door open for the Inspector.

"That's a joke. Your appetite is in full throttle twenty-four seven!" replied the Inspector good-humoredly.

Nora Clark welcomed the Scotland Yard detectives with sincere, warm greetings. Before she had a chance to escort them to a table, Ginny and Liz were at her side grabbing menus and angling with each other to show the officers to a table.

"Can I bring you some coffee or tea?" asked Ginny smiling shyly.

"I just made a pitcher of fresh orange juice," chimed in Liz showing brilliantly white teeth.

"We have pancakes with fresh blueberries this morning," continued Ginny.

"You should try the bacon omelette!" beamed Liz.

"It all sounds great. I guess I'll start with some coffee and a glass of orange juice, the pancakes and the omelette," replied Rogers smiling pleasantly.

"That's it? Couldn't you decide on a few more dishes?" remarked the Inspector, already feeling a twinge in his stomach. "I'll have some coffee and hot oatmeal and bring some fresh cream with that please."

Finishing their breakfast at the Tarts and Buns the police officers headed to the local butcher's to interview Charlie Billers' assistant.

"He's pretty cut up over Edith Kramer's death and it seems genuine if somewhat hostile. I can understand his mood, I mean losing someone who was beautiful, kind, considerate and all around wonderful is a bitch" said Rogers as he and the Inspector left the butcher shop.

"He'd be a fool if he didn't act like the bereaved lover. He says they didn't know each other for very long but even so I find it curious how little he knew about her and can anyone be that wonderful?" replied the Inspector, his nose twitching.

"Did you see his expression when you told him that he would have to give evidence at the inquest? It'll be interesting to see him on the stand."

They were stopped in their tracks by Charlie Billers who had come out of his shop to walk alongside them. "Sorry officers, didn't want to interrupt you but that boy's taking this real hard. He didn't know the poor lady very long but I can tell you he was head over heels in love."

"What was your opinion of her?" asked Rogers.

"I didn't know her all that well, only when she'd come here to talk to Mitch. The little I know is what I picked up from my wife. Seems Ms. Kramer made quite a few enemies around here," chuckled the butcher.

"Did your wife mention anyone in particular?" asked the Inspector.

"Nah, I've learned not to listen. You know how women talk; if they're not whining about something they're nagging about something else. And when two of them get together no one's safe from their wagging tongues. You should hear them when they come into the shop! It's all I can do to get their attention so I can get on with my business. But I wouldn't have a living if it weren't for them so I have to take the good with the bad," he laughed and turned to head back to his shop.

"Let's move on to this Mrs. Brown. Hopefully we'll get a little more information from her," replied the Inspector his head down against the wind.

"Alright but I sure hope all this activity isn't going to affect her health. She's a little mouse of a lady."

When Mrs. Brown opened the door it was obvious to the two policemen that she was trying her best to contain her emotions.

"This is terrible...such a shame...poor lady. I hope she didn't suffer," she prattled nervously as they followed her to the living room where an electric fire burned in the grate.

Politely turning down an offer of fresh scones and tea, much to his Sergeant's disappointment, the Inspector began the interview.

"We don't want to disturb you more than we have to Mrs. Brown, we'd like you to tell us anything you know about Ms. Kramer."

"I'm afraid I don't know very much. She appeared on my doorstep two weeks ago saying she got my name from Lynn Griggs, the postmistress. She was very friendly - you know how Americans can be. She had a very vibrant fashion style. Not what you see everyday, especially here in Epping, but I suppose that's how all Americans dress."

Further questioning revealed that even with all her chatter the extroverted Ms. Kramer had kept her private life private and except for the fact that Mrs. Brown could now recite endless facts about the state of Texas, she knew very little about the dead woman.

"Your offer to drive Mrs. Brown to and from the inquest was very gallant but at the rate we're going we'll need the gypsy's crystal ball to give us any information on the victim," said the Inspector.

"Be careful what you wish for, Inspector. Last but not least on the list are the Leslie sisters," replied his Sergeant grinning.

Cornelia sat at the kitchen table sipping her coffee as she watched her sister's ministrations over scrambled eggs.

"Don't mean to be picky but you've used up an entire bunch of parsley and a basketful of mushrooms on four scrambled eggs. I can't understand why you're so fidgety," said Cornelia.

"I've already told you a dozen times. I feel *awful* saying all those terrible things about Edith.

Don't you understand? My wish came true! Did she *have* to come to Epping Village to get killed?" replied Susana miserably. Then in a more desperate tone said, "Oh dear, do you remember what Martha said about what she'd do to Edith?"

Cornelia's face became sheet white but in an effort to calm her sister's agitated state said, "Now don't panic. You know Martha is always saying meaningless gibberish. One minute she's angry and the next she's laughing hysterically. And I've told you a dozen times that *everyone* in the village wanted to kill Edith. Besides, you make it sound like Epping is Whitechapel and there's a Jack the Ripper lurking behind every tree. Let's not mention Martha to the police just yet. In fact I'm going to tell Pinkey the same thing."

A loud clap of thunder resonated through the room followed by the sound of an upstairs shutter banging in the wind. Almost immediately the doorbell rang.

"I'm sorry you had to come out in this weather. Come on back to the kitchen and you can warm yourselves with some nice hot tea – or do you prefer coffee?" said Susana anxiously leading the police officers to the warm kitchen where her sister sat tending her mug of coffee.

"Mmm, there's always a delicious aroma of home cooking at Blandings." exclaimed Rogers gratefully accepting a mug of coffee.

"You've always had a good appetite, Mikey," laughed Susana. "I just turned some scrambled eggs into something resembling a potted plant but I'd be happy to make you breakfast. What would you like?"

"Thanks Mrs. S., it's a tempting offer but we just had breakfast," replied the Sergeant, not missing his superior's grimace. "Actually we're here to find out anything you can tell us about the deceased, Edith Kramer."

"Oh but we know nothing - do we?" said Susana unwittingly.

"You must excuse my sister's discomfiture, Inspector. She's very upset by these developments. What Susana meant to say is that you have been given misinformation because Edith Kramer is... er...was a complete stranger to us," added Cornelia firmly.

"So you had never met Edith Kramer before?" asked the Inspector.

"Of course not! Oh, it's all my fault - isn't it?" said Susana, making the policemen take notice.

For the second time in only a few minutes her sister was again forced to come to her rescue: "Edith Kramer sat next to us and introduced herself at a Women's Institute meeting a couple of weeks ago.

Susana was, as usual, overly friendly and Edith attached herself to us. Prior to that we had never seen or heard of her."

"That's right. I'm sure she was a very nice person but...I wish I hadn't said all those mean things about her! It looks bad, doesn't it?" sobbed Susana.

Cornelia was starting to feel like an aggrieved defense attorney in a decidedly sordid case with a singularly stupid client.

"Edith Kramer was an intrusive newcomer to the village, Inspector. And the fact that she purported to be a close friend of ours resulted in our being snubbed by the villagers," she ended somewhat feebly.

The interview ended with a polite notification that the inquest would be held later that afternoon and they would be expected to attend.

CHAPTER SIXTEEN

Thanks to what was known as the 'village telegraph', the news of the inquest travelled at hyper-speed, resulting in a large crowd of onlookers gathered in front of the town hall, which among its many functions was also the site of legal proceedings.

"There's Mike Rogers helping Mrs. Brown up the steps. She looks more frail than I remember," said Cornelia as the sisters walked across the green towards the hall.

"You'd look that way too if a murder was committed right under your very nose – wouldn't you?" replied her sister with dismay.

As the sisters approached the hall the frosty treatment from the villagers changed to awkward smiles and sheepish greetings.

"They're speaking to us again, isn't it odd?" whispered Susana after taking the first seats they could find in the crowded room.

"Hm, I wonder what they're up to. It's not in them to change their stubborn mindsets so quickly," replied Cornelia cynically.

The inquest was called to order under the able guidance of an elderly local judge whose stern yet judicious approach was typical of his generation. First came the testimony from the teens who found the body followed by Constable Jenkins, Mrs. Brown, Mitch Harris and the Leslie sisters. Testimony from the lay parties was brief and inconclusive with the exception of Susana's whose incoherent and excitable ramblings completely disconcerted everyone in the room including the venerable judge.

From there the proceedings took on a more serious, technical turn with the testimonies of the professional parties. As chief medical examiner for the county, Dr. Goodman was called upon to give his findings.

Dr. Goodman had lived so long in the village and was so much a part of the everyday lives of its residents, including marrying into an old family, that they overlooked the newcomer appellation.

In his trademark modulated voice Dr. Goodman spoke solemnly and with authority, "Upon immediate examination at the site of Epping Pond, the body was found to have had blunt force trauma to the back of the head. However the fact that it was in water, asphyxia due to aspiration of fluid into the air passages had to be ruled out. This can cause problems because the findings in an autopsy diagnosis of drowning can be cryptic or even absent. In the present case, none of the typical signs of drowning were found. The nose and mouth were free of froth, nor was there froth in the lungs or air-passages; the presence of weeds, stones, and such were not found clutched in the victims' hands; the lungs were not water-logged nor was there water in the stomach or intestines. Immersion in water can aid in determining the time of death as it did in this case. It was determined that the body had been in the water for not more than two hours prior to being found - between eight and ten o'clock in the evening. Even though a minute amount of water *was* found in the victim's lungs *may* still *discount* drowning because it is not uncommon for a person who is under water to asphyxiate from lack of oxygen i.e., holding their breath. Because the body was face down in the water and there were no perceivable foreign objects or injuries to the front of the head or torso, it would appear that the victim did not injure herself upon impact.

Notwithstanding the tests which are being done by the Scotland Yard Crime Lab, it is my professional opinion that if in fact the victim was rendered helpless prior to plunging into the water death could be construed as homicidal in origin."

The subdued tone in the Hall ended with the doctor's last sentence when the crowd burst into excited murmurings. Knowing his fellow neighbors' predilection for gossip the crafty judge decided not to waste his breath asking for order but instead called Chief Detective Inspector Alistair Bunson of Scotland Yard to come forward. This produced the desired effect and almost immediately the room once again settled into respectful silence as the crowd strained to hear the testimony from the esteemed Scotland Yard representative.

The self-effacing Inspector did not take long to state that due to inconclusive medical findings and pending Scotland Yard forensic reports, an extension in the investigation to determine the cause of death of Edith Kramer would be requested.

The request was granted and the Hall was quickly emptied as excited villagers rushed home to have their tea and to impart the juicy news to family and friends.

"No sense in delaying the investigation until we hear from the lab. From the looks of things this is a surefire homicide. Set up an interview with the chairman… er… chairwoman of the W.I.," said Bunson

"Petra Aleman," replied the Sergeant.

"Huh?" uttered a confused Bunson.

Rogers looked at his superior with raised eyebrows, "The Women's Institute chairwoman, Inspector. My mum said she took over after Julia Peters' death."

"Are you telling me we need to interview your mother to get any information?" asked the older man.

"Nah, my mum's visiting her dad in Scotland. I'm house sitting for her," chuckled Rogers. Looking over he noticed his superior's nose twitching.

Cornelia and Susana weren't the only ones making a beeline from the inquest to the teashop. When they arrived the shop was buzzing with happy customers.

Nora Clark walked over to the sisters, "Augh, another murder in Epping Village. Folks are sayin' Scotland Yard will be arrestin' the murderer in one shake of a lamb's tail," she said feigning displeasure.

"Really? I certainly didn't get that impression from Inspector Bunson. In fact it seemed to me that the ruling was inconclusive until they get more forensic information," replied Cornelia mildly.

"Oh I do hope they find that she decided to go swimming and hit her head on a rock and drown… fell unconscious. It's so dreadful to think that there's another murderer loose in the village - isn't it?" observed Susana with a shudder.

Changing the subject Cornelia said, "I haven't had maple-walnut squares in ages. I'll limit myself to two with a cup of green tea."

"All I could think about during the inquest was what I was going to order for tea. I'll have a raspberry tart and an assortment of your delicious tea sandwiches – and Lady Grey tea, please. Thinking about food always has a calming effect. Don't you think so, Nora?" replied Susana feeling better with the prospect of tea.

"Why that's exactly what I always say, Mrs. S.! Food is nourishment for body *and* mind. Is it true that you were good friends with the deceased? Sorry about the way she was found. Funny how she seemed all flashy and tacky, didn't really seem your kind. Ah well, poor soul's in a better place," surmised Nora shaking her head as she went to get their tea.

Susana's face fell as she said "Nora's right you know, what happened to Edith was horrible. She wasn't the most charming person..."

She stopped in mid-sentence when Ginny passed by their table carrying a tray laden with an assortment of mouthwatering pastries.

"Let's not talk about depressing things when we can concentrate on tea, shall we?" said Susana delightedly.

CHAPTER SEVENTEEN

Following the inquest the Inspector and Sergeant Rogers sat in the Chief Constable's office discussing their course of action over mugs of hot, black tea.

"At this point we know of only Mrs. Brown and Mitch Harris as the only people who had a close relationship with the deceased. Harris states that he was at the butcher shop helping Charlie and Alice Billers with the last minute preparations of the catering for the Masquerade Ball and Mrs. Brown says that she was at home watching an old movie," said the Inspector.

"It'll be a real stretch pinning a murder on old Mrs. Brown. Funny that Harris never mentioned

Edith Kramer's obsession with the gypsies at his interview. We might try to get some information from them although they can be quite hostile to authorities," observed Rogers. "That brings up Martha's peculiar interpretation of Macbeth. Seems to me that she's being influenced by those gypsies. You know she's as zany as the rest of the Jenkins'. Talk in the village has it that she has 'second sight'. I don't mind saying that this case is going to take a lot of finesse if we ever want to find a solution.

"I agree. According to the U.S. authorities, the deceased has no criminal record. I hate to say it, but it looks like we might have to ask the Leslie sisters for assistance," conjectured the Inspector, searching his jacket pockets for the indispensable green tablets.

At Blandings, Cornelia and Susana were in the kitchen plating the dinner that Pinkey had prepared earlier.

"Too bad Jack and Ann decided to stay in the City. We're going to have a huge amount of leftovers," said Cornelia.

"That man didn't let Pinkey know til she was almost done with the cooking. I wonder where Martha could be? I'm starting to really get worried because Pinkey doesn't know either. I wonder if the police have found out anything?"

As the sisters were taking plates and silverware to the dining room the telephone rang.

Cornelia went back to the kitchen to answer and when she came back she was carrying an extra place setting.

"That was Inspector Bunson saying he'd like to discuss something with us so I invited him for dinner and surprisingly he accepted. Unusual for him, don't you think? I mean it's out of character for him to socialize when he's working," said Cornelia thoughtfully.

"Oh, that's wonderful! So nice that he's decided to dine with us. That will take care of any leftovers, don't you think?" exclaimed Susana cheerfully. Then in a tone of dread she added, "Maybe he's here to interrogate us about Edith or maybe he's made up his mind that I killed her! Oh dear, I can practically hear the cell doors clanging, can't you?"

"Don't be silly Susana. Edith's death hasn't been formally designated a homicide," replied her sister somewhat absent-mindedly. "And remember not to say anything about Martha!" she ended just before a car could be heard pulling up the drive.

"I'm sure you've been wondering about my being here," began the Inspector once they were seated at the dining room table. "Actually, the reason is somewhat convoluted in that..." "Yes, we know Inspector, but shouldn't I have an attorney present?" interrupted Susana dejectedly.

"I don't quite understand but I'm sure if you'd like an attorney present it would be perfectly acceptable. However I would prefer that you hear what I have to say before you decide," replied Inspector Bunson wondering what had possessed him to interview the Leslie sisters without his Sergeant.

Susana sat silently folding and unfolding the napkin on her lap trying not to look at the food in front of her while trying to imagine the kind of meals served in jail.

Noticing Susana's discomfort, the Inspector softened his tone, "It's indeed an honor for me to dine at the home of such a celebrated chef. In my professional capacity I would not permit myself this pleasure but I am here to ask you ladies a favor. So you see my visit is both social and professional."

"We're delighted to have you here, Inspector," replied Cornelia sending her sister an *'I told you so'* look.

"You're sure I don't have to take a ride with you to the station?" asked Susana timidly. When she received an amused shake of the head from the Inspector she continued, "Oh, then it's our pleasure to have you here, Inspector! Try the broccolini, it's locally grown. It's so nice to live out in the country and be able to get such fresh produce, don't you agree?"

Cheered that her sister was in her usual good 1 spirits, Cornelia quickly said, "Please go on with what you were saying Inspector, of course we'd be happy to do whatever we can if at all possible."

Looking relieved the Inspector said, "I'm very grateful. You were very helpful when...er...we last met. I realized then that your familiarity and knowledge of the workings of the village were invaluable to the solution. I will confess that at this time we do not have irrefutable evidence that Edith Kramer was murdered but it seems highly probable that we will get that finding in the next twenty-four hours."

Cornelia sipped her wine and listened attentively while Susana's earlier inhibitions evaporated and she happily focused her attention on her plate.

The Inspector continued, "This time around your assistance is even more indispensable because of the fact that so little is known about the victim, and frankly, Scotland Yard is finding resistance from the village inhabitants. None of the people we have interviewed have given us any substantive leads to go on. We know that Edith Kramer spent a couple of weeks in Epping but no one is willing to give us any coherent information. Indeed the village, to use an American phrase, has circled the wagons. Someone is being shielded and we need to find out who and why. In other words, we need you ladies to disentangle the village web."

CHAPTER EIGHTEEN

The Inspector was unaware of the anguish he had unknowingly instilled in the two women. For several minutes after the exit of the Scotland Yard Inspector the sisters suffered through a series of vacillating emotions.

"Do you think he was trying to tell us something?" asked Susana with pangs of conscience as they drank their Ovaltine.

Cornelia was too wound up to sit in her usual chair. Instead she paced back and forth in front of Susana's bed. "I was thinking about that while I was changing and I've decided that he definitely was not hinting at anything. When he said the piece about *'shielding someone'* I think he was referring to the closed mouths of the villagers. In other words he wants us to mix in with our neighbors and get information that might not otherwise be obtained solely by the efforts of the authorities," said Cornelia with a flourish.

Leaning back with a sigh of relief and popping a chocolate in her mouth Susana responded, "I'm so happy I'm not Scotland Yard's prime suspect that I'll do anything to help. We'll just have to go undercover and use our superior detective skills to apprehend the kill…er…culprit, won't we?"

"And how do you propose we go undercover?

We're not exactly strangers in these parts. And if you mean wearing trench coats and fedoras, Halloween was two nights ago," countered Cornelia as she continued her pacing. "Recall that the vicar came here to voice his concerns over ugly rumors just a few days before the festival. We know that the village women tend to go to him whenever they have something troubling them so tomorrow we'll pay him a visit and enlist his help. He might give us at least an idea of where to begin our investigations. Afterwards we'll go see Mrs. Brown and hope that she'll tell us more than she told Scotland Yard. I'll call them in the morning and make the arrangements." And with that parting comment she headed for the door.

The next morning the village of Epping awoke to a blue sky and bright sunshine giving a false hope of warmth following the raw, biting cold of the previous few days. During breakfast Susana's attempts to downplay the sunny weather in an effort to dissuade her sister from her habit of walking into the village went unheeded and she found herself in the lane walking at a much faster clip than she would have liked.

"Really, why you must insist on trudging through these lanes when we own a perfectly good car is beyond me," protested Susana pointing to a small wispy mass in the sky. "If there's a torrential downpour and we get soaked and catch pneumonia it'll be all your fault. Could you at least stop walking so fast?" she pleaded while endeavoring to keep up.

Stopping at the crest of the lane Cornelia pointed to the countryside below, now in a patchwork of red, yellow, orange and brown with scattered touches of green. "Why would anyone want to race past this beautiful landscape? It's better than a painting!"

"Alright, let's take a picture and we can stare at it whenever we want. Ugh, my shoes have huge rocks inside them, - don't yours?" retaliated Susana.

"Complaints, complaints, complaints. This is the easy part: downhill. We'll be at the vicarage in ten minutes."

"That's not what's worrying me. If this is the easy part then the climb back will be the *hard* part, won't it?"

The vicarage was situated on the village green adjacent to the twelfth-century Norman church of St. Mary's. It was not uncommon to see large motor coaches full of tourists snapping photos of the church. Invariably they would spill over into the vicarage gardens that were renowned throughout the county for their purity of old English roses. It was Vicar Thomas Peters who planted and maintained the grounds with the help of a part time gardener who did the heavy lifting and mowing. The cemetery behind the church was lovingly tended and hardly a blade of grass was out of place.

When the Leslie sisters arrived at the Victorian house, which had the dubious fame of being the ugliest and chilliest house in the village, the vicar came to the door.

"This sunshine is wonderful! We're so lucky to have such mild weather so late in the year," said the vicar ushering the sisters through the icy corridors to his sunroom. This was one of only two rooms in the expansive house that didn't cause frostbite. The other was the kitchen overseen by the friendly and very chatty Scotch housekeeper, Mrs. Hardy.

"Yes, we were just commenting on the very pleasant weather. Every time I come into this room I'm astonished at the flowers you're able to grow in here!" declared Cornelia entering the sunroom.

"Is Mrs. Hardy not feeling well, Vicar? I haven't run across her in the village lately. She's not ill, is she?" asked Susana with concern.

"She's not ill, thankfully. Just visiting a sick sister in Scotland for the past few weeks. She very kindly asked several of the village ladies to help with meals so there's always someone coming or going with casseroles," chuckled the vicar.

"We've been thinking about your visit to us a few days before Halloween. You seemed very concerned about the stories that were circulating amongst the women," ventured Cornelia.

"Oh you know how these villagers can be.

They're good people but they can be stubborn and narrow-minded. There's nothing new with the spite and gossip that goes on between the women.

However it seemed to me that the dynamics of the gossip took a sudden and nastier turn. Since the sad incident last year I'm trying to be more attune to that aspect of human nature," said the vicar in his tremulous voice.

The cell-phone in Cornelia's purse chirped. The call lasted only a few seconds but it was enough time for the others to notice the changed expression on Cornelia's face. "Edith Kramer's death is now formally classified as a homicide," she said dully.

"So you mean we really have to do this detective work?" gasped Susana involuntarily.

A look of astonishment came over the vicar and Cornelia was quick to explain, "Inspector Bunson seems to think that Susana and I are in a unique position to garner information from the villagers. Unfortunately we're, at this time, not in the best of favor with the women. For some reason or other they're under the impression that we were long-time friends with Edith Kramer and they refuse to believe otherwise. So we thought we might come to you for help."

If possible, the vicar looked more confused, but aware that a response was expected he haltingly said, "I'd be happy to help in any way I can, of course." The vicar's face seemed to crinkle and tugging at his collar he said, "What I am going to tell you might come as a shock but the village gossip is of one mind in that they believe...," his sentence was left unfinished as voices were heard in the hallway and Alice Billers and Petra Aleman entered the sunroom.

"We just popped your lunch in the oven, Reverend Peters. So nice to see you, Cornelia and Susana," said Petra smiling.

"And dessert's in the fridge. Charlie's got some nice short ribs in the shop, Susana, perfect for these cold nights. I'll tell him to save you some."

"Isn't it such a relief to know that we're back in the villagers' good graces?" expressed Susana on their way to Mrs. Brown's house.

Cornelia turned a worried face to her sister. "I wonder what's going on behind our backs."

"Oh, but Cornelia dear, you forget we're assisting Scotland Yard so really there's nothing to worry about - is there?" replied Susana soothingly.

Before the Leslies had time to ring the bell the door was opened by Mrs. Brown speaking excitedly, "Oh how nice to see you! Such unpleasantness these last few days. I've made some nice scones that are just about to come out of the oven and I have a jar of Mrs. Hardy's strawberry preserves from the summer harvest out on the table," she prattled eagerly leading the way to the kitchen.

Setting the tea and scones on the table, Mrs. Brown spoke in a hushed tone, "Mike Rogers and the Inspector from Scotland Yard were here asking about Mrs. Kramer but I had to tell them that I really know very little about the poor woman. I felt badly seeing the disappointment on their faces but I couldn't very well tell them lies! But between you and me her sole interest in life was to have a good time."

"She didn't tell you anything about herself or what she was doing in England?" asked Cornelia.

"Well that's just it, she was *always* talking. I've never known a person who could talk nonstop like that one. The funny thing is that she never said anything."

"Did she have any visitors or did you happen to see anyone with her?" persisted Cornelia looking over at her sister for help. Unfortunately, Susana was too enraptured with the warm scones and strawberry preserves to pay any attention to idle chatter.

"She kept odd hours. But I believe I *did* see the boy from Charlie Billers' shop waiting outside a couple of times although I can't be sure. And now that I think of it I saw another fellow come pick her up but I don't remember what he looked like because he didn't get out of the car. I was cleaning the dining room window," replied Mrs. Brown.

Cornelia persevered, "Do you remember the type of car he was driving?"

Mrs. Brown gave a chirpy laugh, "All cars look exactly alike to me but I believe it was a blue color. But I suppose it could have been black. It was very late and I was just getting into bed so I really can't say."

"Being a newcomer you'd think she'd have questions about the village, wouldn't you?" said Susana wiping crumbs from the table.

"Oh yes, she was very interested in the village! Wanted to know about practically everyone.

Where they lived, what they did. She got a big kick out of our Halloween Festival too. Every morning she'd sit drinking her coffee and die of laughter telling me about all the cat-fighting in the village. 'This place is a riot!' she'd say. Then she'd talk about Texas. My goodness, each day it would be a different story about all the things she'd done there. She had a funny sense of humor, that one."

"That's terrible - what kind of stories?" asked Susana fascinated.

"Silly things. I didn't pay much attention."

"Well we now have confirmation that Edith Kramer was an all around busybody and a trouble- maker which makes our job all the more difficult," contemplated Cornelia as the sisters walked along the village common.

"Certainly Edith was a loudmouth but I can't believe that anyone would commit such a horrible crime over silly gossip, can you?" replied Susana.

"It does seem somewhat drastic but one never knows. I've just remembered that I need some hand cream," said Cornelia quickening her pace.

Lynn Griggs, who had been flipping through the latest Martha Stewart magazine when the sisters entered the village store/post office jumped from behind the counter and gushed, "How nice to see our village heroines! Is there something special you're looking for? We're so proud of you."

Cornelia and Susana stood dumbfounded staring at the postmistress. Finding her voice Cornelia stammered thanks and a request for hand cream.

Lynn Griggs was on a roll and beaming admiringly at the sisters said, "I can't tell you what a relief it is not to have *that woman* disturbing the peace and quiet we're all so used to. Her behavior was scandalous. And now that she's out of the way we can all settle down to our tranquil lives again."

"Not speaking ill of the dead, she was intrusive and it was very difficult to avoid her exuberant personality, wasn't it?" observed Susana.

"*That woman* would steam-roll you as look at you. The *trouble* she made for everyone! She had best friends at each other's throats with the lies she spread. Petra Aleman and Patti Stevens weren't speaking and Alice Billers told Nora Clark she wasn't welcome at the butcher shop because of a rumor that Nora had said that Charlie was selling beef from mad cows. And of course we all thought, wrongly, I must admit, that you two were best friends with her. Then there was all the fuss amongst the menfolk. They didn't really speak about it but we women knew something was wrong and it was that woman who was at the bottom of it all," replied the postmistress expansively.

"Are you kidding?" asked Susana, her head spinning.

Lynn looked around the shop and in a conspiratorial whisper said, "No one was safe from *that woman's* venom," she stopped for effect and continued quickly, "Do you know that she told Patti Stevens that her costume was way too young for her?

'Mutton dressed as lamb' was how she put it. Patti could have killed her."

"How awful! What was the costume?" asked Susana almost on cue.

"Little Bo-Peep. Now mind you she did look just a teensy weensy bit silly with the big pantaloons and the curly blond wig but none of us would ever have said that to her face," replied the postmistress sententiously.

Pleased at her enthralled audience, she continued, "And then she made fun of poor Petra Aleman's costume calling it cliché and boring. She had Petra in tears and she refused to wear it to the Masquerade Ball. Had to have Madam Sonia make her a whole other costume from scratch."

"Did you happen to see Edith any time that evening?" asked Cornelia in a matter-of-fact tone.

"Thank heavens no! I was perfecting my chili and I had Griggs taste-testing all day. We dropped off the chili practically at the deadline, stayed to see the Jack-O-Lanterns and then rushed home to get ready for the Ball. As chairwoman of the Costume Committee there was a lot of overseeing to do so I purposely got to the Hall two hours prior to the official start of the Ball, which would make it about seven o'clock."

CHAPTER NINETEEN

The Scotland Yard detectives were in their office when they received a call from Cornelia Leslie informing them of the day's interviews.

"Sergeant Rogers was telling me about Martha's speech on the night of the murder. It seems that it was an ominous portent with astonishing accuracy," replied Inspector Bunson. "There's even talk that she was more than a little infatuated with the butcher's assistant, Mitch Harris. I don't think I need to tell you that that places her in a precarious situation," said Inspector Bunson feeling a little ill at ease.

"You're not saying that you think Martha murdered Edith Kramer, are you? Because if you are you're completely mistaken. You know she's hare-brained and addled just like all the Jenkinses, but just like all the Jenkins' she's incapable of anything malicious." replied Cornelia with some feeling.

"With all due respect the phrase *'person of interest'* comes to mind. However in deference to your invaluable assistance we'll refrain from using that offensive expression," countered the Inspector.

"Please don't arrest poor, dear Martha. We'll keep her under house arrest at Blandings. We won't let her out of our sight, will we Cornelia?" cried Susana with helpless sincerity.

Inspector Bunson silently agreed with the Leslies that premeditated murder was not in Martha's character. But as a representative of Scotland Yard it was his duty to keep an objective outlook. "Alright, I'll depend on you to watch over her," he said, feeling a twinge coming from the area of his stomach.

Not unexpectedly, the Inspector and his Sergeant met with resistance when they ventured into Hunter's Bosk to interview the gypsy Yarko. Yes, he had read in the paper of the death of Edith Kramer but with all the people visiting the camp it was impossible for him to remember ever having seen much less talked to the woman.

Leaving Hunter's Bosk Sergeant Rogers gave a sigh of exasperation, "He's obviously lying but all his papers and permits are in order so we can't even use intimidation to get any truth out of him."

"Did you notice Zora watching us without any pretense?" asked the Inspector.

"Yeah, although I had a feeling she was paying more attention to what Yarko was saying than to us," replied the Sergeant. "By the way, how did you know that was Zora?"

"Hollywood couldn't have done a better job typecasting her," chuckled the Inspector.

"Bruce Lingstrom isn't due at the station for at least one hour. How 'bout we go grab some lunch at the Raven's Roost?" suggested Rogers expectantly.

Forty-five minutes later the Inspector winced as he got into the car and immediately popped the ever-present green tablets into his mouth, "Did you *have* to order that second plate of fish and chips? I was enjoying my soup until then," he said morosely.

Back at the police station and seated comfortably in front of his computer Rogers observed, "I have a couple of Lingstrom's writings here. Looks like he's into the latest fad of organ meats and raw eggs. Wouldn't have thought he'd be interested in plain old chili if he likes to eat that stuff."

"Please spare me the gory details," replied the Inspector grimacing in pain. "Just my luck, I'm practically doubled over with gastroenteritis and I have to interview another foodie."

A few minutes later a knock on the door brought the food writer looking somewhat disheveled and wearing dark sunglasses.

"Sorry about my appearance, had a bit of an accident on my way here. Thought I'd take advantage of the fine weather and take a walk in Hunter's Bosk but I must have strayed off the path and wound up lost," he said rather sheepishly.

"Yeah those woods can be tricky if you don't know your way around," replied Rogers, taking in the wet patches on the writer's pants.

"I'd brought a packed lunch from the Raven's Roost thinking I could write a piece on the joys of picnics in the English countryside but to top things off I slipped on a slimy rock as I crossed a small brook. I could feel my left eye swelling even before I got up," replied the writer taking off the sunglasses and revealing a brightly colored and very swollen eye.

"I hope you still had your picnic, the food from the pub is some of the best around," said Rogers, dismissing the injury and focusing on the more important subject.

"Unfortunately it flew out of my hand and landed squarely in the water. But I agree, the food at the Raven's Roost is surprisingly good. Considering its size, Epping Village has some excellent cooks. I had a difficult time choosing the best chili recipe."

"Really? I mean I read some of your articles and I was more than a little surprised that you'd come out to the country to judge a chili cook-off," replied Rogers.

"Hey, I have to make a living and a food writer can't get stuck in the past. It's really similar to the fashion industry. Have you seen photos of runway shows? Who wears that stuff anyway? Only the outrageously rich. Same goes for food. Would the average person really want to eat a black egg that has been lying around fermenting for a hundred 142 years? It's a status symbol in some circles, and we food writers make a living selling that drivel."

"Huh, makes sense," replied the Sergeant as his superior steadfastly focused his gaze on the trees outside while trying to keep his lunch down. "You chose Edith Kramer's chili as the best out of all the entries. What was so special about hers?"

"Most of the entries were quite good but that particular entry had finely diced potatoes, something I'd never tasted in chili previously. In my opinion they not only added extra texture but really enhanced the flavors of the spices."

"Sounds delicious," said Rogers, eliciting a faint moan from the direction of Inspector Bunson.

"Of course some chili aficionados like to add green peppers while others like big pieces of garlic and..." a loud groan from the Inspector silenced the food writer.

Realizing that it was time to change topics, Rogers quickly asked, "Had you ever met the deceased prior to this week?"

The food writer looked defiant. "Never. Look, I know I'm in a curious position by an unfortunate coincidence but before you go making up your minds that I had anything to do with that woman's death, I want you to know that the judging was absolutely above board. In fact the chairwoman of the W.I. had the tasting at the Town Hall with no one except her, the vicar and myself present. I had no idea which chili belonged to whom."

"We'll have to find out if a packed lunch was prepared from the Raven's Roost and if anyone saw him on his walk," said Inspector Bunson when the food writer had departed.

Returning to Blandings Susana once again perseverated over Martha. "That Martha is so infuriating! If we hadn't known her all our lives I'd be frightened to death of her, wouldn't you?" said Susana as she and Cornelia took their lunch into the dining room.

"She certainly does have one too many chinks in her armor but I don't think she's capable of hurting anyone – at least not consciously," replied Cornelia.

"So you think she could have coshed the Kramer while in some kind of fit?" stammered her sister.

"I really can't say. Do you remember how she came into the ballroom on the night of the Halloween festival? She was in one of her trances. I'm not a shrink but don't people who are in a hypnotic trance do things they don't remember later? We'll have to ask Dr. Goodman about that."

"Ugh, too horrible to contemplate. Don't you think left-over brisket makes delicious sandwiches?" replied Susana, wiping a spot of mustard on her chin.

Poking her head through the door, Pinkey said, "Sorry to bother but Mrs. Billers is here saying she just has to see you. Shall I tell her you're having lunch?"

Alice Billers came in with two bright red spots on each of her cheeks. "I'm so sorry to bother you while you're at lunch," she said breathlessly. "I normally wouldn't have barged in on you but I felt that I needed to tell you…er…thank you for what you have done for the village."

The sisters exchanged mystified looks and stared at Alice.

"It's nothing really. We're only trying to…," began Cornelia but she was interrupted by more gushing from the butcher's wife. "Really, how can you both be so modest! You embody the true noble spirit of selflessness. To think that you would put yourselves in harm's way to help the village. It's just too wonderful!"

"Thank you Alice but it's our pleasure if it helps in clearing up this ghastly business. Why, in a way we enjoy it – do you really think we're in harm's way?" replied Susana letting a pickle drop from her hand.

Alice beamed and said, "You and your modesty again. But I do have to say that some of the women are still upset about the costume thing and one or two are still stinging from the chili outcome but thanks to you that's all going to be forgotten!" The sisters could only exchange bewildered looks.

That evening after a hastily prepared supper owing to Pinkey's date with her latest beau which she *'could not possibly put off'* the sisters decided to go to bed early and hash over the day's developments.

"Are you alright Cornelia? You hardly said a word all through dinner. I hope it wasn't the sardine sandwiches. I might have added a little too much of the *Coleman's* mustard. Or maybe it was the olives?"

"The sandwiches and olives were fine. I just can't figure out why the villagers are so congenial all of a sudden after almost not speaking to us for weeks," replied her sister settling back on the divan.

With obvious relief Susana said, "Yes, I thought the sardines particularly delicious and the rosemary bread from the Tarts and Buns is perfect with sandwiches. Which reminds me, I think there's some leftover *Panna Cotta.* Want to go down and get some?"

"N-no thanks," said Cornelia still somewhat distractedly.

Disappointed, Susana said, "I don't see why you're so suspicious of the villagers. They know we helped solve the last mystery in Epping and they're grateful that we've volunteered our services with this new case. It's obvious - isn't it?"

Yawning, Cornelia got up and said, "I'm not so sure. But in any case I can't think anymore. See you in the morning." And with that she went to her room and got gratefully into bed.

CHAPTER TWENTY

In their eagerness to help Scotland Yard, the Leslie sisters awoke early in preparation for the business of 'interviewing' the locals. Just as they were about to leave the manor they picked up a call from Sergeant Rogers informing them that the police had received word from Charlie Billers that Mitch Harris had not been to work for the past two days and that an investigation of his apartment revealed a hasty departure.

Despite being ensconced in the warmth and comfort of a car safe from the dark clouds and icy wind, the sisters' mood mirrored the outside elements.

Susana shuddered, "A murderer...loose in the village...shouldn't we do something to warn everyone?"

"The village telegraph will take care of that, Susana," replied her sister distractedly.

"But aren't our investigations? Clearly Mitch Harris is the murderer - isn't he?" asked Susana in a quavering voice.

Glancing at Susana's anxious expression Cornelia continued in a more upbeat tone, "Mikey said to continue until further notice. The best way we can help the villagers is by doing what we do best - snooping. We've perfected the art and will use it to the best of our ability!"

"Don't you think we're being a little devious going around with a pretext of canvasing a 'Bring and Buy' sale at Blandings?" asked Susana, wrapping her woolen scarf tightly around her shoulders.

"With the customary high efficiency of the village telegraph they'll be expecting us with hot tea all ready and waiting," replied Cornelia trying to sound cheery.

Petra Aleman's house was set in a small development of houses, in a cul-de-sac on the edge of the village. Cornelia parked in front of an immaculately landscaped garden midway down the cul-de-sac and admired the still green lawn and meticulously trimmed shrubs. At the side of the house were the remains of what must have been, until just recently, a brilliant display of flowers. A stone path bordered by neatly arranged flowerbeds led to the front door.

Susana rang the doorbell to the sound of a German cuckoo clock.

"I just heard on the radio that a nor'easter is headed our way. I'm afraid we'll be in winter before the end of the day!" said Petra as she ushered the sisters into a brightly lit entry hall. A cozy fire could be seen in the living room and the smell of freshly baked pastry filled the air. "Sit in front of the fire and I'll be back with the tea things."

The sisters were comfortably settled by the warmth of the fireplace when a furry animal with soulful eyes came trotting in and sat next to Cornelia.

"Oskar! You remember me! Or is it food you're after?" laughed Cornelia, affectionately petting the Schnauzer.

"That rascal will take anything off your plate before you know it's even there!" laughed a tall gray haired man. Ron Aleman was a retired engineer and RAF pilot.

"Don't mean to intrude but I promised Oskar I'd take him on a long walk and I'd better do it before the weather changes."

Petra came in carrying a plate of *Apple Streudel* torte full of apples, pecans, cinnamon and brown sugar. "This is a family specialty," said Petra, handing each sister a plate. Now tell me about the 'Bring and Buy'. I'm so indecisive about what to bring to a

B&B. I never think anyone's going to want whatever it is I bring. But I can always find something I just can't live without!"

"You have such lovely things Petra, I would think anything you bring would be snapped up immediately! Isn't that right Cornelia?" replied Susana looking around the pleasant room.

"Yes, and I can't part with them! I wind up going out and buying something to bring!" laughed Petra.

"It's all for a good cause with the proceeds going to charity so everyone benefits. Interestingly there's usually not many things left over – except of course whatever Lady Millicent brings," giggled Cornelia, eliciting similar responses from the other women.

"The torte is positively scrumptious, why not bring this?" expressed Susana approvingly while forgetting that the 'Bring and Buy' was just a ruse.

Quickly changing the subject Cornelia said, "Speaking of food, you entered the chili cook-off, didn't you Petra? We heard that it was a difficult contest to judge with all the great entries."

Petra's face turned bright pink and a few seconds passed before she spoke. "Yes, but I knew I wasn't going to win because there are so many other people in the village who are much better cooks."

"Now that's not true. You're a fantastic cook and you know it. I've never tasted something you've made that hasn't been outstanding, have I?" said Susana with a mouthful of torte.

Petra abandoned the airy tone and spoke more solemnly, "I guess it doesn't matter since an incomer won the contest. And to think we all thought you were friends with her! She really had us fooled with talk that she knew you in the States. I couldn't understand how you put up with her boasting and her claims that she knew how to do everything better."

Cornelia suppressed a laugh remembering Edith's bragging that everything was bigger and better in Texas. "We're all in agreement, Edith Kramer was a pain in the neck. But she suffered a gruesome death deservedly or not," she said.

"But she *did* deserve it!" responded Petra impulsively. "She practically ruined the Halloween Festival with her lies!"

Susana sat up in astonishment, holding her fork in mid-air two inches from her mouth. "What kind of lies?"

Her voice quavering, Petra said, "She actually had the nerve to tell me that there was talk that I was purposely going to show up Lynn Griggs by wearing the same costume! And when I tried telling Lynn that I had no idea what her costume even looked like she didn't believe me. I was dumbfounded when I found out that she was going as *Druzilla* from '*101*

Dalmations'. Later we found out that Edith had given her the idea knowing that Madam Sonia was making that costume for me!"

"It doesn't seem like Madame Sonia to be making two exact costumes for two different people - does it?" said Susana vaguely.

"Of course not!" replied Petra shrilly. "Poor Madame Sonia was caught in the middle! She had no idea that Edith was spreading vicious lies. We never found out where Edith got the information about the costumes-definitely not from Madame Sonia. But at the time we didn't know that and so we all secretly blamed her. I feel so badly about that."

"Do you remember seeing Edith during the festival? I realize you must have been terribly busy as W.I. chairwoman," asked Cornelia casually.

Petra laughed and said, "Are you kidding?

Edith made her presence known wherever she went! The Chili Committee decided that in fairness to all the contestants, a small batch would be taken from each entry and a number was assigned to the bowl. No one except Reverend Peters knew which bowl belonged to whom. When Edith showed up at Town Hall to deliver her chili she was incensed that she wasn't allowed to put her name on the bowl and she made everyone know it. The vicar managed to calm her down. Unfortunately Lynn Griggs entered the room just as Edith was leaving. Edith screwed up her nose and made a comment that she'd never heard of chili smelling like curry. Lynn was fit to be tied when she heard that remark. After that I didn't see Edith again. I was with the vicar and Bruce Lingstrom until about six o'clock when we all went over to the Jack-O-Lantern lighting ceremony. Of course Ron was also with me for most of this time."

"You'd never convince me that either Petra or Lynn could commit murder. Do you think they could really hurt anyone intentionally, much less kill them?" asked Susana emphatically as Cornelia backed out of the Aleman's driveway.

"Highly unlikely but you never know what someone is capable of doing if they get pushed to the brink," replied her sister. With a sigh she continued, "Patti Bounty is next on the list. Don't you have a book on order at the library? We can use that as an excuse to speak with her."

Except for the bun at the back of her head and her penchant for wearing twin sets Patti Bounty did not fit the stereotypical mold of a librarian. She was always eager to engage visitors in conversation, albeit in whispers, and she had never been seen or heard putting her finger to her mouth and uttering a 'shush'.

When the Leslies walked in Patti was stacking the latest magazines.

"Just the person I wanted to see! The book you signed up for has just been returned. You're going to enjoy it," said Patti in her usual friendly way.

"The author has me in stitches from cover to cover with all his books. I can't wait to start reading his latest. Although we have a lot of detecting... Susana stopped short when she noticed her sister's scrunched up face.

"I heard you might be coming by to talk about that silly Edith Kramer and I can understand your need to talk about her but I want you to know that she got what was coming to her. She was a pushy, manipulative slut and everyone in the village was sick of her," replied Patti.

"Hmm, she definitely wasn't a saint. Strange how she found pleasure in taunting people. Practically every woman in the village has a story," remarked Cornelia cagily.

Patti Bounty gave a mirthless laugh, "*Both* sexes were fair game with her. You should have seen her performances at the Raven's Roost. The minute she'd walk in the women would leave. For the first time in thirty years my husband came home completely blotto because of her," she finished with resentment.

"You must have seen quite a bit of her since you're such good friends with Mrs. Brown," continued Cornelia.

"Not really, she spent a lot of the time out and about doing her mischief. The last time I saw her was on the evening of the Masquerade Ball," replied Patti.

"What time was that?" asked Cornelia excitedly.

"Well, Andy and I were at the chili cook-off and then around six thirty I went along to Millie's with my chili since she didn't go to the festival. The hussy was there jabbering about how everyone would react when she made her grand entrance at the Ball with the winning costume. I wasn't going to stay and listen to her gibberish and besides, I had to get ready for the Ball myself, so I put the chili in the fridge and left. Then I went over to Alice Biller's around seven o'clock so we could work on last minute details of my costume. Andy picked me up at eight."

The 'detecting' was cut short when the sisters received a call from a distressed Pinkey with news that she had found a note from Martha.

As they pulled up on the gravel drive they could see Pinkey waiting with Martha's note in her hand. The young woman looked to be on the verge of tears. After Pinkey's call the sisters had been silent, afraid to utter the thought that was foremost on their minds. Now they quickly went to Pinkey with comforting words that sounded hollow in their own ears.

"Pinkey dear, we must not presume too much.

Mikey, that is, Sergeant Rogers told us expressly to continue our..."

She was hastily interrupted by Cornelia, "I think we should calmly read Martha's note before we start theorizing," she said, a million thoughts racing through her head. Cornelia took the torn half sheet with the scribbled writing.

> "Gone to do importent stuff.
> Martha"

"You know your Aunt Martha, is daffy but she knows how to take care of herself. You know that, don't you?" said Susana feeling a flood of relief knowing that it was in fact Martha's

"Uncle Billy's on his way over," said Pinkey.

Excellent, he'll know what to do. How about if we sit down with a nice cup of tea while we wait for your uncle?" replied Susana pulling out a tin of shortbread from the cupboard.

It was not long before Billy Jenkins drove up in the company of Inspector Bunson and Sergeant Rogers.

Rogers spoke kindly to Pinkey, "We've put out a description and Constable Jenkins has notified the various agencies so we should have word on your aunt's whereabouts very soon."

In the meantime, the Inspector was in the library speaking to the Leslies.

"At this point we don't have any idea where Martha could be or if she's with anyone. And in my opinion, she's un-balanced enough to do almost anything."

"Do you think she's been kidnapped?" whimpered Susana.

Neither Cornelia nor the Inspector responded resulting in Susana sobbing quietly into a large handkerchief.

After politely emphasizing to the sisters the need to continue their investigations now more than ever the Inspector rejoined the others and they left with an offer to drive Pinkey home and which she gratefully accepted.

CHAPTER TWENTY-ONE

That evening Jack and Ann returned from the City and were distressed to hear the latest news about Martha.

"I guess it's the Raven's Roost tonight. Kill two birds, as the saying goes. Dinner and a chance for you to do some clandestine detecting," said Jack after hearing that his sisters were once again helping Scotland Yard.

"Please, Jack, try *not* to use gory descriptives at a time like this, will you?" said Susana blowing her bright pink nose.

The wind had been fierce for much of the afternoon and now it was virtually howling. By the time the Leslies arrived at the Raven's Roost the pub was already packed with the usual crowd of villagers happily chatting at the bar, glad to be inside near a roaring fire. As per routine, the Leslie women grabbed a table while Jack went to the bar for the drinks. A short while later, they heard someone call out from the direction of the bar. Turning they saw Charlie Billers grabbing Jack's arm.

"There's some that think because they live in a big house they can push people around," snarled the butcher.

Jack disengaged himself from Charlie's grip and walked away while several men shouted at the butcher.

"What in the world happened back there?" asked Ann as Jack handed out the drinks.

Jack shrugged, "Don't know but he's one sip away from being dead drunk."

"I told you not to use that word, Jack! Don't you remember?" pleaded Susana just as Charlie Billers' wife Alice appeared at their table.

With some hesitation she said, "Sorry about what just happened, Jack. I don't know what's come over Charlie lately. It's not like him to pick fights. I'm thinking it's the stress over Mitch that's getting to him. Please don't mind him," she finished self-consciously.

"Already forgotten, Alice," replied Jack with a smile.

Just then Bert Colby appeared holding menus.

"You picked a good night to join us. The wife has some nice specials," which he proceeded to describe with exhuberant detail.

While the rest of the party was absorbed with Bert, Alice Billers took the oppotunity to whisper to Cornelia. "I'd like to speak to you and Susana privately."

"Meet us at the Tarts and Buns at nine tomorrow morning," Cornelia whispered back.

"Stella certainly has expanded her repertoire and everything sounds delicious! The *Cioppino* would be perfect for a night like this but the *Turkey Cannelloni* sound good too. What do you suggest?" said Susana her brows furrowed.

"The *Cioppino* is hearty and full of robust flavors and like you say, perfect for tonight. The *Cannelloni* are light and airy with a white wine sauce.

They're both magnificent. For you, I would say maybe the *Cioppino*," replied the landlord.

"The *Cannelloni* sounds delicious. What about you, Cornelia?" asked Ann as Alice rushed back to escort her husband home.

"I missed the specials when Alice was talking to me. Is there a new chef?" asked Cornelia.

That night with an empty Ovaltine cup, and over the sound of fury outside, Cornelia looked up to see her sister nodding off.

"We still have a few more people to interview.

We should go to Hunter's Bosk and speak to Zora tomorrow," she said turning off the light.

Susana's eyelids fluttered and in a sleepy voice she uttered, "Zora?" Almost immediately the room lit up followed by a loud crack.

The entire night the village was hit by thrashing rain that continued into the morning. When the Leslie sisters arrived at the Tarts and Buns Alice Billers was already waiting at a table in the farthest corner of the room. There was a dish with several pastries and a large cup of dark tea in front of her.

"It was so depressing this morning I thought I'd get here a little early. Help yourselves to the pastries," greeted Alice. She continued in a more flustered tone, "Thanks for coming. I've been so worried about everything that's happened. It's all Edith Kramer's fault; she turned this village upside down with all her carryings on."

"We've gotten that sentiment from quite a few of the women," replied Cornelia as Ginny came to take their orders. When that had been accomplished Cornelia continued, "Had Edith done anything in particular to distress you?"

Alice snickered, "She had a talent for provoking everyone she met! She couldn't see you on the street without coming over with some comment."

"Believe me, we know that quite well, don't we Cornelia?" added Susana, munching on a raspberry bar.

Alice leaned forward and said, "Don't you think it funny that first Mitch disappears and then Martha? And I don't know what to make of Charlie, he's acting like he's scared of his own shadow since Mitch's disappearance. He never drank much and now he goes to the Raven's Roost and comes home completely awash in liquor," finished Alice, her lips quivering.

Pulling out her huge handkerchief Susana uttered. "Yes, we've been worried sick. Too horrible to contemplate, isn't it?"

"Poor Martha, she was head over heels in love with Mitch. But Mitch was completely under Edith's spell. That's what I wanted to tell you. One of the times that Edith was at the shop she boasted that she was having an affair with Bruce Lingstrom. The harlot actually said it in front of Mitch!"

"And his reaction?" asked Cornelia.

Alice shrugged her shoulders, "No reaction that I noticed. Of course he was probably used to Edith's bluster."

"How terrible! Who would want to hurt someone's feelings like that?" offered Susana with a mouthful of carrot cake.

"Sounds very much like Edith," replied Cornelia. "Can you remember if you saw her on the day of the festival!"

"Sure I can, she wasn't a shrinking violet you know. Charlie and I saw her inside the maze in the late morning. She was with Mitch. Then when I saw her next she told me how she was going to take first prize at the Chili Cook-off."

"And did you see her later that evening?" asked Cornelia just as her cellphone began ringing.

Excusing herself she answered the call. Closing her phone she said, "That was Mike Rogers. They've found Mitch Harris' body."

"Oh no! I knew this would happen. Did he say where he was found?" asked Alice feebly.

"He didn't say but it's definitely a homicide."

Alice Billers gathered her purse saying, "I've got to go and see Charlie before he finds out."

"Did you see Edith on the night of the Ball?" persisted Cornelia.

Alice turned back to face her. "No, I was with Patti Bounty altering her costume at my house most of the evening. At the Chili Cook-off Patti came up to me crying, saying that she still didn't feel comfortable with her costume even after Madame Sonia had altered it and asking would I help her with alterations later that evening. She came to the house around seven o'clock and we were hard at work until about eight, when she left. Charlie and I were supplying a large amount of the late night supper for the Ball so we left almost immediately to go to the shop and load the van. Mitch was there to help. We finished by nine o'clock and headed home to get into our costumes and then on to the Ball." Before turning to leave she added, "Thanks for everything you've done, really wonderful of you."

"I can't believe the news about that nice boy.

He was always so polite and helpful. Isn't it a travesty?" sniffed Susana. Then desperately wringing her hands she continued, "What about Martha? Do you think something terrible's happened to her?"

"I hope not," said Cornelia distractedly as she watched Alice and Nora Clark whispering by the front door. "Inspector Bunson wants us at the station in one hour. We'll have to tell him about Bruce Lingstrom and Edith. This keeps getting more convoluted by the second."

In a flash Nora was at their table. "Alice just told me that Mitch Harris was found murdered. It's unbelievable. He was a really wonderful person," she said looking like she was Susana got up and putting her arm around Nora she said, "Sit down, Nora. Ginny will bring you a cup of strong tea, won't you Ginny?" Ginny hurried and fetched a large mug of tea for her employer.

After a few sips Nora regained her composure.

"That Edith Kramer has caused so much grief. Mitch would be alive now if it hadn't been for her and who knows what's happened to Martha?" She stopped to take another sip and continued, "Alice just told me that now she knows that I never said that

Charlie sold beef from mad cows. That Edith had the women of the village at each others' throats with all her lies."

"Including us! That was her M.O. causing rifts between friends. I think she enjoyed it - don't you?" replied Susana.

"Your shop was open during the festival isn't that right?" Cornelia asked Nora.

"Yes, on the day of the Halloween Festival we always get a lot of customers and we do a huge take out business. I don't like to deny Ginny or Liz their fun so I ask them to work until one o'clock in the afternoon and then it's just me and my assistant, Otto, until at least nine o'clock at night. Otto is elderly, somewhat of a grouch and doesn't care for any recreation except baking, so I left at nine to get ready for the Ball. Norman picked me up at a quarter to ten."

"I guess we won't have time to go to Hunter's Bosk and speak to Zora, will we?" asked Susana hopefully as the sisters walked into the police station.

They were immediately taken to the small office where Inspector Bunson and Sergeant Rogers sat looking through various papers.

"Have you found Martha?" asked the sisters in breathless unison.

"We haven't located her yet. But I hope you know that we're doing everything possible to find her," replied Rogers.

Inspector Bunson cleared his throat and added, "The body of Mitch Harris was found in a meadow on the north side of Sam Taylor's farm. The perpetrator had tried to hide the body by throwing hay on top of it. One of Sam's foremen found the body this morning. I don't need to tell you that this case has gotten especially dangerous." Swallowing a couple of his green tablets he continued, "We appreciate all you have done to aid the department but the risk of putting you in harm's way necessitates that we call off your assistance."

Both women looked stunned. Cornelia was the first to speak. "Thank you, Inspector, we appreciate your concern. However..."

"I'm sorry, Ms. Leslie but this is not up for discussion. We thank you for all you've done and implore you both not to take any unnecessary risks," interrupted the Inspector with a half-hearted smile.

"If that's how it has to be I guess there's nothing we can do. However there is one last thing we have to tell you, Inspector. Today we learned that Bruce Lingstrom and Edith Kramer were having an affair," replied Cornelia leaving the Scotland Yard detectives with their mouths hanging.

"The nerve! Taking us off the case. Why, I've never been fired from a job before - have you?" said Susana with indignation as they got in the Rover.

"You don't for one minute think that we're going to stop do you? We're getting valuable information that the police will never obtain no matter how hard they try. No, we're carrying on our own investigations. We've done it before and we can do it again," replied her sister, her mouth set in a tight line.

CHAPTER TWENTY-TWO

Sergeant Rogers shook his head as he looked at his computer screen. "I still feel badly about dismissing the Leslies. I know their safety was at stake but we took them by surprise. That family is looked up to in the village and for good reason.

Which leads me to believe they're not going to allow a murderer to go rampant in Epping."

"For their sakes, I hope you're wrong," replied his superior.

"Yeah, I know," replied the Sergeant with a frown.

A knock on the door alerted them that as per instructions Bruce Lingstrom had been picked up and was politely shown into the room.

The food writer looked agitated. "I was told that you needed to speak to me. Couldn't you have used a phone? You had to have me picked up?"

"Thanks for your cooperation, Mr. Lingstrom.

Mind telling us what you've been doing the past couple of days?" asked Rogers ignoring the other's question.

"As I told you I did not murder Edith Kramer but I have no problem telling you that for the past two days I've been working on a story about British pubs and their cuisine. I got the idea from the other time you had me in for questioning."

"So you've been at the pub for the past two days and haven't gone anywhere else?" asked the Sergeant.

"No, I've been taking day trips to other pubs in the area. I can give you names and numbers if you'd like. The woman was killed a few days ago.

Why do you want to know about my activities of the past two days?"

"What were your relations with the murdered woman, Mr. Lingstrom?" asked the Inspector, ignoring the writer's question.

"I told you that I had never met her before the festival, Inspector."

"You didn't see or speak to her prior to the festival?" asked the Sergeant.

The writer looked ruffled, "I might have spoken to her at the pub. Yes, I remember that she came up to me and introduced herself. She was already more than a little blotto by then and bragging about her chili. I must have blocked that memory. It wasn't a pleasant experience."

"So what were your relations with the deceased?" asked Rogers.

"I told you, no relations except for the Chili Cook-off. She might have said something when she dropped off her chili but there was so much activity with people coming and going with their entries that I didn't much pay attention. You can confirm all this with Mrs. Aleman and the Vicar. I didn't see or speak to her again."

"Alright. Thank you for your time and if you'd leave all your information at the front desk we'll keep in touch. By the way, if you plan any more day trips we'd appreciate your letting us know in advance," said the Inspector.

"Another rumor going around the village or the guy's a convincing liar," said Sergeant Rogers when the food critic had left.

"Yes, we'll have to keep a close watch on Mr. Lingstrom," replied his superior.

"It's getting late Cornelia, we'd better postpone going to Hunter's Bosk until the morning, don't you agree?" asked Susana as Cornelia drove towards the gypsy camp.

"It's only dusk and there's still plenty of daylight left, Susana. Anyways we won't be there very long. We haven't yet spoken to Zora and now that we're working independently we'll have a talk with Yarko."

"I don't think that's such a good idea, Cornelia. Talking to Zora is one thing but Yarko is another. Who knows what he might do. He might be the murderer and we'll be walking right into his hands! Do we really have to go?" gulped Susana.

"Good grief, you've got to stop watching those late-night movies," replied Cornelia as she parked the car.

Susana looked warily around her. Then with forced gaiety she said, "Oak trees are so majestic.

Although they do have a sinister look about them when it's raining - don't you agree?"

Aware of her sister's uneasiness Cornelia replied, "It's stopped raining and I smell something delicious. Look, there's the gypsy camp! It looks so friendly with the people talking and milling around the campfire. Maybe we can get something to eat," she finished somewhat disingenuously.

Mollified, Susana picked up her pace, "It does smell good. I think it's beef stew. And it looks like wine is flowing too. Isn't it a beautiful setting?"

Once inside the camp the Leslies stood looking around for the hold gypsy woman. The gypsies continued with their lively talking and eating but every once in a while they stole furtive looks at the two women.

"Can I help you ladies?" came a man's voice directly behind them. His thick accent conjured up vivid thoughts of Bela Lugosi.

"Yarko...hello...yes...we'd like to speak to Zora...if possible," replied Cornelia in little gasps.

Yarko gave a little bow and walking away said, "Come, I will take you to her."

"If he puts on a black cape I'm out o' here, you know?" whispered Susana.

Yarko walked up to an old caravan. Before he reached the steps Zora appeared at the door. "Come, we will go to the tent," she said to no one in particular as she passed by them.

Inside the fortuneteller's tent the candles were lit but the crystal ball was no longer in the center of the table. Instead, a copper bowl was set over a candle. Also on the table was a small leather pouch.

"We'd like..." began Susana but she was stopped midsentence.

"Do not speak until I tell you," interrupted the gypsy as she lit the candle and proceeded to take out what looked like laurel leaves from the leather pouch.

Slowly, she placed the leaves one by one into the bowl while quietly reciting an incantation. Susana and

Cornelia strained to understand what she was saying but to no avail. Presently an aromatic smoke rose from the bowl. The gypsy stood over the bowl with her eyes closed and continued with the incantation.

After a couple of minutes she picked up a pitcher and poured water over the leaves. After swirling the leaves with one hand she gazed intently at the mixture in the bowl. The swirling and gazing were repeated three times.

Lifting her eyes to the two women in front of her, Zora began, "When you were here last I told you there was evil in Epping but you did not heed my warnings. Martha communicated to the entire village the evil that was at hand, but again, no one listened.

Now it is too late. Two are dead and before long there will be one other who will meet the same fate."

Susana squealed and putting a hand over her mouth asked, "Wha...what... d...do you m...mean?"

"The leaves show there is one other who is in great peril. That is all I can say," replied the old woman as she blew out the flame under the bowl.

"Do they tell who might be responsible?" asked Cornelia, surprised that she would be taking the divination seriously.

Zora gave a short, stereotypic cackle and said, "Our people have learned not to go past a certain point with our powers. " Then she got up and pointed to the exit where Yarko was conveniently waiting.

"That was...enlightening...thank you," said Cornelia feeling more confused than ever.

"Will you join us by the fire and have some wine?" offered Yarko charmingly.

"No, thank you, we have dinner waiting, don't we Cornelia?" replied Susana with an appealing look at her sister.

Feeling slightly mutinous and avoiding eye contact with her sister, Cornelia replied, "Actually we'll go to the Raven's Roost for dinner – too late to start cooking so we'd love to join you."

Susana gave her sister a withering look. By now all the gypsies were gathered around the fire drinking and talking gaily. As soon as Yarko approached the fire a group got up and made room for him and the two women. Another brought them goblets of wine.

Taking advantage of the moment Cornelia asked, "Yarko, what do you make of all that's happened in Epping lately?"

Almost instantly the clamor of laughing voices stopped, replaced with dozens of startled, dark stares.

"Edith Kramer was a bad woman. She was not good for this place. We gypsies tell her she is not welcome at our camp. We try to stop selling to her but she makes a big scene and says she will call the police. She says she will tell them that we steal money from her. So instead we try other ways to keep her evil away."

"What other ways?" asked Cornelia, vowing to herself that this would be the last thing she'd ask tonight.

"Gypsy ways," replied Yarko.

CHAPTER TWENTY-THREE

A sudden flash of lightning followed by a clash of thunder enhanced the atmosphere of doom that pervaded the ride back to Blandings as the strain and tension of the past couple of hours came to a head. The sisters sat in silence each oblivious of the other and immersed in her own thoughts.

Presently the scrunching of gravel on the driveway made Susana sit up and with a forlorn sigh she said, "It'll be our fault if anything's happened to Martha. We should have kept her locked up in her room. There's a lunatic running around loose in Epping and we're no closer to finding a clue than when we first started. I want to scream with frustration. Why don't the police do something?"

Feeling equally powerless, Cornelia ignored the question and with more conviction than she felt said, "It does seem like everything's a jumble but there's got to be some clue in our notes that we've overlooked. In the morning let's review the notes again and make a timeline. I'm sure we'll find something to give the police."

A steady rain began to fall with resonating thunder and lightning as the sisters walked into the kitchen.

"I certainly don't feel hungry but I wouldn't mind a stiff drink before bed, how about you?" said Susana.

The next morning feeling both mentally and physically exhausted Cornelia came out of her room and slowly descended the stairs. In the kitchen she found Susana at the kitchen table with only a cup of coffee in front of her.

"I guess you didn't sleep either," observed Cornelia dully.

"I don't feel like drinking this coffee much less eating anything. Does that answer your question?" countered Susana.

"Sorry it's so awful. I should have listened to Jack when he said my coffee tastes like potato water," said Ann coming in just in time to hear Susana.

"No, no, the coffee's excellent. It's just that Inspector Bunson told us he didn't want us working on the case anymore and then the gypsies told us we're responsible for the murders - devastating isn't it?" replied Susana glumly.

"I'm sure the Inspector had good reason to take you off the case. Something like *safety* perhaps? You two have to get it into your hard heads that it's best to mind your own business," said Jack, studying the coffee pot.

"You forget, dear brother, that Susana and I have a successful record of solving homicides for Scotland Yard," responded Cornelia loftily.

"Actually it was only one homicide - wasn't it?" added Susana.

"We're not giving up on this case. We intend to go over our notes again and..." began Cornelia.

"Maybe some fresh blood, sorry for the bad pun, can pick up something you haven't. Jack and I have nothing to do this morning and I'm sure we'd be happy to help, " offered Ann enthusiastically.

The Leslies spent the rest of the morning meticulously reviewing notes and making a timeline on the night of Edith Kramer's murder.

TIMELINE

PETRA ALEMAN:
5:00pm – 6:30pm: Chili Cook-off
6:30pm – 7:00pm: Jack-O-Lantern lighting

7:00pm – 8:00pm: Administrative duties
8:00pm - Left for home with husband
10:00pm – 2:00am: Masquerade Ball

PATTI BOUNTY:
6:00pm – 6:30pm: Chili Cook-off
6:35pm – 7:00pm: Mrs. Brown's house
7:10pm – 8:00pm: Alice Biller's house
8:15PM – 9:45pm: Home
10:00pm – 2:00am: Masquerade Ball

LYNN GRIGGS:
6:00pm – 6:15pm: Chili Cook-off
6:30pm – 8:45pm: Home
9:00pm – 2:00am: Masquerade Ball

ALICE BILLERS:
6:00pm – 6:45pm: Chili Cook-off
7:00pm – 8:00pm: At home fixing Patti' Bounty's costume
8:15pm-9:00pm: With Charlie at Butcher Shop
9:00pm-on: Town Hall helping Petra w/set-up and Ball

MRS. BROWN:
5:00pm-6:30pm: Home cooking dinner
6:30pm-7:00pm: Patti Bounty comes over with chili
7:00pm-on: Home

178
"Dr. Goodman put the time of death between eight and ten o'clock in the evening. Has it occurred to you that everyone on this list had the opportunity to be at the scene during that time?" asked Jack with eyebrows raised.

"It doesn't make sense, Jack, because the only person who doesn't have an alibi for those times is Mrs. Brown and I'm not inclined to think that she would actually murder anyone," said Cornelia somewhat doubtfully.

"And Mrs. Brown insists that she saw Edith during that time. So that supports everyone's alibi!

Doesn't it? Or does it?" said Susana in her typical obtuse thinking.

"She's positive that Edith was in her room getting ready for the Ball. Mrs. Brown might be elderly but she has all her marbles," replied Cornelia firmly.

The discussion was interrupted as Jack left the room to answer the ringing of the doorbell. He returned with Inspector Bunson and Sergeant Rogers.

"Sorry to disturb you without calling first but I thought you might be interested to know that Alice Billers was found..."

"Another murder?" shrieked Susana voicing what the others were thinking.

"Not quite, but almost. She had a knife wound that missed her heart by fractions. We're just coming from the hospital."

"How did it happen?" asked Jack.

"We don't know yet. Petra Aleman found her lying face down in the pond and immediately called for help," replied Sergeant Rogers.

Looking squarely at the Leslie sisters, Inspector Bunson said, "We're here primarily to advise you that if you hear or know of anything that might put you in danger you must notify us immediately instead of trying to investigate on your own. We hope you don't need any more proof that the perpetrator or perpetrators of these crimes aren't playing games."

After the police officers had left, Jack spoke out forcefully, "That settles it. This is where the display of detective play-acting ends. You heard what they said. You're liable to be killed!"

Any fight Cornelia had evaded her and in a grim voice she said, "I suppose you're right."

"Well now that that's all settled I'll cook up a nice breakfast for us. We could all use some nourish- ment after everything that's happened. Why would Charlie Billers want to kill Alice?" said Susana thoughtfully.

Events of the past several days were mulled over during breakfast with everyone having different views and opinions. In the end they came to an amicable decision to agree to disagree.

"Do you have any errands to run today?

Because I'll be happy to tag along if you do. I need some exercise after that ginormous breakfast," said Cornelia to her sister.

After looking up at the ceiling for inspiration, Susana responded, "N-n-n-o..."

"Good. We'll leave in five minutes," replied Cornelia before her sister could think of a reply.

A few minutes later when the Rover passed the center of the village Susana stammered, "Where are we going that you're in such a hurry...wait a minute, you're up to something, Cornelia, and if it has anything to do with all these murders you can let me out right here. Are you nuts?"

"You want to get out of the car here? Right in the middle of Hunter's Bosk?" asked Cornelia feigning innocence.

"Ohhhh, I guess I have no choice. It's bad no matter what. *Where* are we going anyway?" groaned Susana.

"We're going to pay a visit to Alice Billers," replied Cornelia, waiting for the onslaught.

"You've answered my question. You've definitely gone over the edge. Alice is in the hospital! Actually she might be in the morgue by now. And besides, the Inspector told us she had a guard by her door. We'll never make it past the front door - will we?"

"Well then we'll just have to use our little grey cells to find a way to speak to her," replied Cornelia with a sly expression.

CHAPTER TWENTY-FOUR

Upon entering the hospital and being told that Alice Billers was not allowed visitors the Leslie sisters turned as if to leave and then headed in the direction of the patient's room.

Providentially they found Constable Billy Jenkins slumped against the door. It didn't take long for the sisters to convince the gullible policeman that as Scotland Yard operatives it was imperative that they speak to the patient.

Once inside the room it was clear the patient had suffered a serious injury. The left side of her chest was heavily bandaged and she was covered with the usual invasive apparatus. She lay as if asleep, the dark circles around her eyes intensifying the pallor of her face.

Cognizant of their compromising situation, the sisters stood awkwardly in front of the bed. Susana played with her bracelet in nervous agitation until it slipped off her wrist. Bending to retrieve the bracelet she banged her head against the bed, waking the patient. Fear registered on the patient's face. The shock of being brutally attacked was evident in the blank look in her eyes.

In a panic, Cornelia threw caution to the wind and asked the victim if she had seen her attacker. At first Alice only stared wide-eyed at Cornelia, the dark circles around her eyes seemingly darker. Then shaking her head and sobbing quietly, she murmured, "I don't know, I don't know."

The Leslie sisters didn't stay long enough to provide comfort to the sobbing Alice. They were out in the hall telling Constable Jenkins that on no account was he to mention their visit to anyone and within five minutes of leaving Alice's room they were speeding towards the village of Epping.

"We'd better call Inspector Bunson because if Jack hears about this we'll be wishing we had a nice warm cell in which to hide. I almost broke an ankle running to the car. We're acting like we're the maniacs, aren't we?" said Susana trying to catch her breath.

"No, we're not maniacs. We're doing what the police can't do. They don't know Alice Billers like we do. They'll believe her when she says that she doesn't know who attacked her."

"Poor Alice, what an awful thing to go through. I got the impression that she was covering up for her husband. I only hope Martha's all right. The police would have told us if anything…has happened to her - wouldn't they?"

As if on cue, Cornelia's phone rang, startling both women. It was Sergeant Rogers letting them know that Charlie Billers had been arrested for the attempted murder of his wife. The knife used in the attack had been found with his fingerprints near the scene.

"Does that mean he's responsible for the two murders?" asked Susana after the first throes of shock and disbelief.

"The police are going to go through their routine but we'll find out soon enough," replied a resigned Cornelia.

"He'd better tell them where he has Martha or I'll go to the station myself and beat it out of him, the big brute! Wait, maybe we should both go?" said Susana anxiously.

I think we should have dinner at the Raven's Roost tonight, said Cornelia pensively.

The village pub was in a flurry of activity when the Leslie party walked in. With all tables taken the Leslies were left standing shoulder to shoulder around the bar. The only topic of conversation was the arrest of Charlie Billers with heated opinions loudly expressed by all.

"You picked a great night to come to the pub, Cornelia. If we don't get a table soon we'll be forced to eat standing up," said Jack recovering from an unintended shove and avoiding having his beer spilled all over the front of his jacket. Turning in search of a place to sit he spotted a familiar figure walking towards a table hidden from view.

"I think we're in luck. Careful with your drinks and follow me," pronounced Jack, heading in the direction of the figure.

The familiar figure turned out to be Sam Taylor sitting alongside an attractive middle-aged brunette. Also seated at the table were Dr. and Mrs. Goodman. Upon seeing the Leslies, friendly greetings and introductions were exchanged and they were urged to join the party. The woman with Sam Taylor was a divorcee from the next town over who had recently boarded her horse at the Taylor farm. She and Ann immediately struck up a conversation.

Falling into a chair Susana said, "Thank goodness Jack saw you! I couldn't have stood another second with all the jostling. Isn't it awful about Alice and to think her husband was the butcher! Yikes, that's a spooky coincidence - isn't it?"

"He hasn't been charged yet, Susana. It's an involved process the police have to go through before a person is formally charged with a crime," replied Dr. Goodman.

"Oh dear, I was hoping they'd caught the murderer and all this dreadful business would be over - are you sure?" said Susana in an about face.

"If Edith Kramer's death took place between the hours of eight and ten o'clock at night then according to Cornelia and Susana's timeline, there are several people who had the opportunity," said Jack.

"I'm just the coroner, Jack. I perform the autopsies and give an approximation of the time of death along with the cause of death. In the case of a homicide where no weapon is found I make an interpretation of the wound and it's cause. Of course, there are cases where the homicides are remarkably alike and one can presume that the same person committed them – with forensic backup, of course. In the case of Edith Kramer, she was hit over the head with a rock that we believe the killer threw back into the water. The lab found that the cause of death was due to a violent blow to the head and that she was dead before she fell in," replied the doctor.

"The paper quoted you as saying that Mitch Harris died from blunt force trauma to the head – just like Edith. However Alice was stabbed and she must have known her killer because, correct me if I'm wrong, she didn't have anything under her nails, nor were they chipped. Could there be two murderers running around Epping?" suggested Cornelia.

"Certainly. But that's not my area of expertise," said the doctor gravely.

"From the evidence it doesn't look good for Charlie," observed Ann, looking up from the menu to find an unusually frazzled Bert Colby making his way to their table.

Wiping his forehead dramatically the pub proprietor stood by the table and said, "Sorry to keep you waiting. It's been a madhouse here since we opened today. Calamities and misfortunes in the village always boost business. We're practically out of everything on the menu. But don't panic! In my personal refrigerator I have a couple of lasagnas that I would be happy to share with you. That and a nice green salad and you'll have a feast!" exclaimed the loquacious landlord. Not waiting for their reply he hastened to the kitchen. In a matter of minutes he reappeared with their meal, which in truth did look mouthwateringly delicious.

"There must be a pound of cheese on my plate alone!" said Jack, trying to get a long string of melting Mozzarella cheese into his mouth.

"Mmm, can you tell that the pasta is freshly made? It's so silky I can cut it with my fork! And look at those slices of garlic in the sauce. Weren't we lucky Bert ran out of food?" said Susana, oblivious of the backhanded compliment.

"I think I heard your phone ringing but I'm not sure with all the noise in here," said Ann to Cornelia.

"It was the vicar," replied Cornelia after checking her phone. "If you'll excuse me I'm going to go outside to return the call."

A few minutes later she returned with a strange expression on her face.

"You're not going to believe this. Reverend Peters was all in a dither because he had forgotten to tell us earlier that the village women are convinced that Susana and I are responsible for Edith Kramer's death! I don't know whether to laugh or scream," she said in vexation.

Dropping her fork which was midway to her mouth Susana practically shouted, "Oh my gosh, you mean they think we killed her?"

"It sounds like that's the universal consensus.

Although it's baffling that Scotland Yard has allowed you two to roam the countryside killing and maiming the residents," chuckled Jack.

"Don't be an '*AssJack*'," said Cornelia, using a childhood insult. "We're not in jail because the women haven't voiced their opinion to the police. Let me see, how did the vicar put it? Oh yes, the women are 'standing firmly on our side and will be forever grateful to us for ridding the village of Edith Kramer.'

It explains the curious change in attitude."

Suddenly a loud guffaw emanated from the kindly doctor. "I'm sorry...couldn't...hold it..." he said covering his mouth again in uncontrollable convulsions. The effect was contagious sending the others into paroxysms of laughter.

Wiping away tears and trying to catch her breath, Cornelia said, "The vicar also mentioned that Zora wants to see us tomorrow morning."

"I didn't know the Vicar was into fortune- telling. Did you?" asked Susana in amazement.

CHAPTER TWENTY-FIVE

The next morning the countryside was bathed in a watery sunshine, giving one the illusion of being inside a watercolor painting.

Zora was waiting outside her tent when the Leslies approached the edge of the gypsy camp.

"Come, we will go inside," she said, motioning them to follow her.

The sisters walked behind the gypsy. While the sunshine wasn't at all very bright it was bright enough that they had to close their eyes to adapt to the darkness inside the tent. Opening their eyes the sisters took a step back and after surprised gasps both cried out, "Martha!"

After the exclamations of wonder were over, Zora asked them to sit down so she could explain.

"Gypsy ways are ancient ways that have been passed down for generations. It is normal for people to feel love, anger, joy, sadness, envy. But we gypsies have the ability to feel evil. You were told many times that there was danger brewing in Epping but you didn't listen. Edith Kramer was at the center of this evil. However, without any proof gypsies do not go to the authorities. Martha spent many hours here at camp watching and listening, absorbing what she could. I see when Edith Kramer and the young man Mitch Harris come to the camp that she has him in a trance. I try to protect Martha from this but she does not comprehend. On the night of the Masquerade Ball I try to explain to her that she must stay away from Edith Kramer because she is a bad woman. When she is killed the feeling of evil continues. After I learn of the death of Mitch Harris I become worried about Martha, I feel the evil coming near to her and so I tell her that if she wants to learn gypsy ways she must stay and live at the camp. We gypsies watched over her keeping her close. I have Martha write a note to you so that you will know that she is alive and we deliver it to your home. Then the butcher's wife is attacked and the butcher is arrested. One evening during the harvest moon when all gypsies feast, dance and tell stories around the campfire

Martha tells a story. It is a shocking story. At first we keep the story to ourselves. It is not the gypsy way to interfere in outsider's business. But now we can no longer keep it to ourselves. I have explained as best I could the events of the past days to Martha and she has come to accept what I have told her. Today she has agreed to tell you her story.

"Good thing we drove! I'm still in shock, aren't you?" whispered Susana behind the wheel of the Rover.

"You can say that again – on both counts!" replied her sister, turning around to check that Martha was still asleep in the back seat. "The Inspector and Mike are due to meet us at Blandings in twenty minutes."

"It's my own darn fault. I had to ask them for help. I should have known that once asked they wouldn't stop," winced Inspector Bunson with a grimace of pain.

"You'll find a couple of bottles of your antacids in the glove compartment, Inspector," replied Sergeant Rogers, anticipating his superior's urgency.

As the Inspector swallowed a handful of tablets Rogers continued, "They're a determined pair, not to mention stubborn. I wouldn't be surprised if they tell us they've solved the case." The Inspector quickly swallowed another handful of pills.

Martha was put to bed with a glass of warm milk and a sedative. The sisters barely had time to wash up and join their brother and sister-in-law for cocktails in the library when Inspector Bunson and Sergeant Rogers arrived.

"Inspector, are you not feeling well?" asked Susana solicitously.

"Let me fix you a drink and we can all hear what my sisters are up to," said Jack going to the bar.

In an aside he added, "I have a feeling we're going to need it." The police officers gladly accepted his offer.

Both Cornelia and Susana looked more than a little ill at ease. In her discomfort Susana sat nervously swirling her glass causing an ice cube to sail through the air just missing Inspector Bunson.

Used to her sister's antics Cornelia faced her audience and said, "Before we begin I want to say that while we appreciated and still appreciate your kind warnings Susana and I both felt that at no time were either of us in any danger." While Cornelia spoke solemnly, Susana assumed a vague expression vacillating between pride and fear.

"For reasons you can obtain later, Zora felt that Martha's life was in danger, so on the night of the Halloween festival, after Martha gave her performance at the Masquerade Ball and went back to Hunter's Bosk, Zora had her stay at the gypsy camp where she kept her hidden. During her stay there, Martha told of a strange occurrence. It seems that on the night of the Ball, with her head full of troubling facts which Martha could not completely understand, she decided to go to her favorite place to *'commune in the moonlight'*. She didn't realize that it was a moonless night that evening. Martha lay face down in a small grove of ferns on the water's edge, contemplating the water when she saw Edith Kramer walking towards the pond and stopping about twenty feet away. She looked like she was in costume and waiting for someone. After a while, Edith walked up to the water's edge and stood looking into the water when she was suddenly hit from behind and then crumpled to the ground. Martha remembers seeing Alice Billers throw something into the pond and then pull the costume off the lifeless Edith and dress her in her own costume – which she had taken off. Looking around, Alice then dragged Edith into the water and stuck her face down beside a dead tree. She then proceeded to dress in Edith's costume and leave. Martha sat there aware of what she witnessed but unable to process her thoughts. After sitting by the water for what must have been close to an hour she came to the conclusion that what she had witnessed could only be the realizations of Zora's premonitions and warnings. At that moment Martha believed that she had gained gypsy insight and that she was destined to be a true messenger of omens. She got up and in a trance of shock and ecstasy walked a few hundred feet to the village green, entered the by then packed Masquerade Ball and delivered her speech. With the commotion caused by the finding of Edith's body Martha tranquilly walked back to the gypsy camp where she stayed until it was decided by the gypsies that it was time to contact the authorities. Or should I say Susana and myself?" finished Cornelia with a slight smile.

If the room was quiet when Cornelia was reciting Martha's story, it was in complete and utter stillness when she finished. Her audience was in a shocked stupor.

"It takes your breath away, doesn't it?" said Susana gratuitously.

Mike Rogers sat with a wry smile on his face, nodding in agreement. He waited for his superior to speak.

"Again you've proved your ability at detecting. You've done an exceptionally nice job, ladies. Of course you realize that it's all hearsay and can't be used in a court of law," remarked Inspector Bunson. Then with a kindly smile said, "Undeniably, you've given us very valuable information which we'll use when conducting further investigation. We'll need to speak with Martha. Where is she, by the way?"

"She's locked up in her room, nice and safe – and drugged. At least I hope so. One can never tell with Martha, can one?" said Susana uncertainly.

"I'll give orders for a constable to be stationed here. But you ladies were brilliant. Who knows if we'd ever have gotten that piece of the puzzle!" declared Mike Rogers enthusiastically.

"That's an amazing story. Poor Martha's gone through a lot," observed Ann.

You're a pair of incorrigible super sleuths," laughed their brother.

"Those two are impressive, to say the least – aren't they, Inspector?" asked Rogers with a chuckle as he drove to the hospital. Seeing that the Inspector's nose was twitching he quickly continued, "A couple of men from headquarters are standing guard at Alice Billers' hospital room and Charlie Billers is at the station waiting for us."

While Charlie Billers had continually proclaimed his innocence, he refused to talk. However, when faced with the information obtained by the Leslies he literally broke down and gave evidence against his wife. His refusal to speak was due to his remorse over having had an affair with Edith Kramer, maintaining that he had been 'bewitched' by the deceased woman. Edith began to black mail him, saying she was going to tell his wife about the affair if he didn't give her money on a regular basis. Even after he started giving her cash she continued to taunt him. He was a nervous wreck, living in fear that Alice would find out while at the same time paying out blackmail. Alice never let on that anything was the matter so he began to believe that Edith was bluffing. When Mitch Harris was killed he found a bloodied metal mallet thrown in the dishwasher. With Mitch's disappearance he was the only person butchering meat so he was baffled by the presence of a mallet encrusted with blood, besides the fact that it was customary for the butchers to hand wash all their utensils. He was thrown for a loop when a knife from his shop was used to attack his wife. After his arrest his attorney had made it clear to him that his wife's description of the attack along with the weapon used placed him as the prime suspect. It was at this point that he began to look back on the night of the first murder. When he asked his attorney about Alice's interview he was flabbergasted to learn that she had told the police that she had been with him and Mitch the entire time they were making the preparations for the delivery of the food to the Ball. Alice had only been at the shop between eight and eight-thirty that evening. She had told him that she was going to the Hall early in order to help Lynn Griggs with set up and that she would meet him there for the Ball.

Alice Billers sat comfortably in her hospital bed, enjoying a dinner of ready-mix mashed potatoes, an overcooked piece of beef and flavorless, soggy, frozen vegetables. She looked up in surprise as the Scotland Yard detectives walked in, followed by a uniformed constable.

Not bothering with the social graces Inspector Bunson said, "We have information that you were seen at the Epping Village pond at the time of the murder. Constable Morris will take down your statement. We'd like you to...."

"Tell you how I killed Edith and Mitch? I must say I'm a little shocked to see you here so quickly. I really thought I had fooled you," said Alice, continuing to eat her meal.

With the fleeting thought that once again the Leslies were instrumental in solving a homicide, the detectives let the remark pass and carried on with professional detachment after giving the usual warnings.

"Plainly and simply I killed Edith Kramer because she was a conniving bitch. I never cared what she did to the others but when she told me that she was fooling around with Charlie I could have killed her right then and there. I began to plan how I was going to do it and I came up with incriminating the villagers. It was easy with the way she was always boasting and bragging. Of course she did help by telling everyone that she was the best at everything. I was the one who spread the rumors about the Leslies being best friends with Edith – just an extra little touch. I decided that the best time would be on the night of the festival when everyone in the village would be home getting ready. I called Edith and told her that I knew about the affair and that if word got around it would ruin the business. I told her I was bringing her more cash and to meet me at the pond.

She was a greedy slime-ball and I knew she wouldn't pass that up so after helping Patti with her costume. I met Charlie at the shop where we got the food loaded in the van. I told him I was going to help Lynn Griggs with the last minute decorations at the Hall but I went to the pond instead. When I got there Edith was accommodatingly looking at the water with her back to me so I crept along the grass as silently as I could, thanked my lucky stars that there was no moon, picked up a rock and hit her over the head. I couldn't believe how easy it was. I actually thought she was dead right there. I threw the rock into the water and not wanting to waste time I quickly pulled off her costume, which took no time since there was ridiculously little to it, put her in the costume I had come in and dragged her into the pond. I figured if she wasn't dead already she would be by the time I stopped holding her head down. I had brought a mask and her costume had a headpiece with a wig so I went to Mrs. Brown's looking like I had just stepped out of a Las Vegas floor show. When I got there, Mrs. Brown was in her room. I mumbled that I'd forgotten something in my room, asked her for the time and went to Edith's room. I spent time pacing up and down, and opening and closing drawers to establish that Edith was alive and well between nine and ten o'clock at night. I changed into another costume, stuffed Edith's costume in the fire and finally left for the Masquerade Ball, again asking Mrs. Brown for the time.

I'm sorry I had to kill Mitch. I really hated doing it but I had no choice because he had the nerve to confront me with Edith's murder. Apparently Edith had told him, believe it or not, about her affair with Charlie and he decided that I was the likeliest suspect.

He made it very easy for me. I knew he jogged after work on a regular basis so I took a mallet from the shop and kept it in my car so I'd be ready if I happened to run into him. I made it a point to drive around every evening and sure enough I was driving by Sam Taylor's farm when I saw him. I flagged him down, got out of the car and told him we had to talk. I waited for him to turn around and then I hit him with the mallet. Believe me, it wasn't easy dragging him into that field.

By then Charlie was becoming neurotic and started spending a lot of time at the Raven's Roost. I knew it was only a matter of time before the dope figured it all out so I planned the attack on myself. I decided that after a few days of playing the poor, helpless victim of domestic violence, I would finally succumb to fear and give you the name of my assailant–better known as *my husband*. Knowing how you dopes operate it would only be a matter of time before you decided he was the perpetrator of the other two murders. The planning was the easy part. The actual act took more guts since I have a phobia of sharp objects."

CHAPTER TWENTY-SIX

"To our very own Epping Village detectives!" toasted Phyllis Stavis, pushing up her paper party hat with one hand while holding her glass out to the many responses of "Hear, hear."

The Leslie family and their friends sat in the Blandings dining room, celebrating the American holiday of Thanksgiving. Two tables covered by white tablecloths were placed end to end in order to accommodate the large party. Small vases with bouquets made up of autumn flora lined the center of the tables, interspersed by candles in crystal holders.

The fire in the fireplace was a happy contrast to the early snowfall that had started that afternoon.

The festive scene became even merrier with the popping of Champagne corks.

"I always look forward to your Thanksgiving dinner, it's such a treat for us Brits!" said Sam Taylor enthusiastically. He was accompanied, by the pretty brunette with whom he was now continually seen.

With perfect timing Pinkey walked in, pushing a trolley with three golden turkeys. Susana followed with another trolley loaded with large bowls of cranberry sauce, stuffing made with ground beef and garlic, mashed potatoes made with a gallon of fresh cream and a pound of butter, platters of broccolini, sweet potatoes loaded with brown sugar, butter, pecans, and topped with roasted mini-marshmallows, and platters of sliced heirloom tomatoes with sliced oranges, red onions, Nicoise olives and drizzled with a lime vinegrette. The Leslie childhood favorite, Jello pudding, was also served.

Well into the meal and with plenty of red and white wine flowing, Susana asked, "I guess Zora was talking about Alice when she said *'Another will meet the same fate'*. I wonder how she does it?"

"Alice was found to be criminally insane so she'll spend most of her life in a sanitarium," replied Inspector Bunson.

"That's too bad. Of course it was a little frightening having a killer loose in the village. And poor

Charlie's taken all this so badly - I wonder who our new butcher will be?"

"What I'd like to know is how Edith was able to get all the low-down on the costumes. A lot of us were keeping our costumes secret," said Lynn.

"I think I'm to blame for that," said Patti Bounty somewhat self-consciously. "You see, the women would be doing research on costumes at the library and asking me to find books on a certain topic for them. I didn't think I was doing any harm telling Mrs. Brown when I'd go visit her since she doesn't get around much. Well, she innocently told Edith and that's how the whole costume thing got started."

"I told you it wasn't your fault Patti, you're a good friend to Mrs. Brown and she was just making conversation with Edith," said her husband.

"I too have a confession," said Petra. "When I was going over the festival ledgers today I noticed that I had inadvertently switched the numbers on Edith and Mitch's entries. The real winner of the chili cook-off was Mitch not Edith."

"That makes sense. I found it hard to believe that Edith ever set foot in a kitchen," replied Cornelia.

"But it was Alice who had all the women believing that Cornelia and I murdered Edith Kramer.

And she seemed so sincere when she was gushing all that sacchariney stuff. I hope she doesn't miss the lamb chops and filet mignons - I know I would. But I wouldn't go on a killing spree either - would I?"

"Help me get dessert, Jack?" asked Ann, noticing that Susana was more than a little tipsy.

They came back with two trays loaded with pecan, apple and pumpkin pies. There were also two bowls of whipped cream.

When everyone was served, Martha got up from her chair and announced that she was going to join the gypsies.

"Do they know that?" asked Cornelia under her breath.

"Know what? If you have any questions about your destiny I'll be ready to answer them as soon as my crystal ball is delivered. I've ordered it special from Zora and she says only the inner circle of gypsies are allowed to gaze at the crystal to obtain knowledge. That's gonna be me soon," Martha preened.

"Martha, I've been admiring your outfit all evening! The colors are dazzling, aren't they?" remarked Susana.

"Yeah, all gypsies wear bright colors and fancy skirts. Only gypsies are allowed to wear gypsy clothes and since I'm almost a gypsy, Zora's gone and given me permission. Anyways they wouldn't fit you," said Martha with a self-congratulatory sniff.

"How did you know my clothes were getting a little tight?" replied Susana, staring in wonder.

"Martha, you're a heroine and we're all so very proud of you," said Mike Rogers.

"Gosh, it weren't nothin'. I was just doin' gypsy stuff," replied Martha, coyly batting her white eyelashes.

SALMON CROQUETTES
(as served at The Tarts and Buns Teashop)

2 lbs. Salmon, chopped
6 scallions, diced
1 1/2 inch piece fresh ginger, diced
3 TBSP fresh spinach, finely chopped
1 egg white
1 TBSP soy sauce
2 TBSP vegetable oil (not olive oil) cooking spray

Pre-heat oven to 175°F.

In a small bowl mix the egg white and soy sauce then in a large bowl combine the salmon and veggies.

Add the egg white and soy sauce and blend. Scoop the salmon mixture (it will seem mushy) and make into 3 inch wide patties.

Spray a pan with non-stick spray. Add the oil. Working in batches, gently but firmly place the patties in the pan being careful not to crowd.

Cook on medium heat for 5 minutes, turn and cook another 5 minutes or until done.

Place cooked patties in oven to keep warm.

Serves 6.

CHICKEN AND CORN CHOWDER
(as served at Blandings Manor)

2 chicken breasts poached and then shredded
1 pkg. ready cooked bacon
6 small Yukon gold potatoes, peeled and cut into bite size pieces
2 15 oz. cans of corn kernels, drained
2 quarts chicken stock
4 cups heavy cream or half-and-half
4 oz. Jack or Muenster cheese, shredded
2 TBSP chopped cilantro
2 TBSP olive oil

Place bacon on a plate covered with paper towels and cook for approx. 1 minute. Put aside until it cools.

When cooled, chop the bacon.

Heat the oil in a soup pot and add the bacon, chicken, potatoes and corn and saute for about 2 minutes.

Add the stock, bring to a boil then reduce and simmer for 20 minutes or until the potatoes are tender.

Add the cream or half-and-half and simmer for another minute. Take off the heat and stir in the cilantro and cheese.

Serves 6

PUMPKIN PIE
(as served at Blandings Manor)

1 9 inch unbaked pastry shell
1 15 oz. can pumpkin (not pie filling)
1 14 oz. can sweetened condensed milk
2 eggs
1 tsp. ground cinnamon
1/2 tsp. ground ginger
1/2 tsp. ground nutmeg
1/2 tsp. salt

Pre-heat oven to 425°F.

Place pastry into pie dish using weights to keep the dough from bubbling and bake for 25 minutes. When done set aside to cool.

In a large bowl, combine all ingredients except pastry shell and mix well. Pour into cooled pastry.

Reduce heat to 350°F. Cover the edges of the pastry shell with foil and bake for 30-35 minutes or until toothpick inserted 1 inch from edge comes out clean.

Cool and store in refrigerator.

Serves 8

CIOPPINO
(as served at the Raven's Roost)

1 stick butter
1 Vidalia onion, chopped
5 garlic cloves
1 bunch Italian parsley
2 15 oz. cans whole tomatoes (with juice)
2 quarts chicken broth
1 bay leaf
1/2 tsp. dry oregano
1/2 tsp. dry thyme
1 1/2 cups white wine
1 cup water
1 and 1/2 lbs. any firm white fish, skinless and cut into chunks (not too small because they will break down in the broth)
1 1/2 lb. fresh crab, chopped
1 lb. shrimp
Italian bread loaf

Melt butter in large soup pot and add the onions and garlic cooking until onion is translucent. Add the tomatoes, broth, wine, water, and herbs. Cover and simmer for 25 minutes. Add the fish and shellfish and return to boiling. Cover and simmer another 5 minutes. Serve with Italian bread.

    Serves 8.

BAKED APPLES NEW ENGLAND
(as served at Blandings Manor)

6 red apples such as Cortland or Empire
3 tsp brandy
6 TBSP maple syrup
4 TBSP unsalted butter, softened
1 tsp. vanilla extract
1 cup heavy cream

Preheat oven to 450°F.

Combine 4 TBSP of the maple syrup, brandy, vanilla and 1/2 cup of water. Set aside. Cut off the top third of the apple scooping out the flesh being careful to leave enough the entire bottom and walls.

Place apples in a large pie dish or a 9" square baking dish. Fill them with the butter mixture and drizzle with the maple syrup mixture. Bake for approx. 1 hour while continually basting the outside of the apples. Let cool for 5 minutes.

Whisk the cream and remaining maple syrup and pour over apples.

Serves 6

MAISON CHICKEN aka *'MY SON CHICKEN'*
(as served at Blandings Manor)

6 chicken breasts w/bone and cut in half
4 slices bacon
1 Vidalia onion, chopped
6 garlic cloves chopped
1 cup white wine
1/2 cup Marsala salt and pepper to taste
1 lb. wide noodles
1 TBSP cornstarch
1/4 cup of water
5 TBSP Italian parsley, chopped
4 TBSP olive oil

In a saute pan cook bacon until crispy. Remove bacon from pan, let cool and then chop. Leave bacon drippings in pan.

Add 2 TBSP of the oil to the pan. Season the chicken with salt and pepper and add to pan being careful not to crowd and working in batches and setting aside on a platter.

When all the chicken is cooked, add the onions and garlic to the pan until transluscent. Add the wine, Marsala, Italian seasoning, bacon and chicken. Bring to a boil, then reduce, and simmer for 30 minutes.

Meanwhile, cook the noodles. When done, drain the noodles and add the rest of the olive oil and stir to coat. Place the noodles in the center of a platter, add the chicken and pour the pan juices over everything. Sprinkle with parsley and serve. Serves 6.

Printed in Great Britain
by Amazon